I0630319

Down in the Flood

Down in the Flood

Stories

Luke Whisnant

Iris Press
Oak Ridge, Tennessee

Copyright © 2006 by Luke Whisnant

All rights reserved. No portion of this book may be reproduced in any form or by any means, including electronic storage and retrieval systems, without explicit, prior written permission of the publisher, except for brief passages excerpted for review and critical purposes.

This is a work of fiction. Any resemblance to actual people, places, or events is coincidental and unintended.

Iris Press

is an imprint of the Iris Publishing Group, Inc

www.irisbooks.com

COVER PHOTOGRAPH: "Bridge," by Peter Groesbeck
www.petergphotography.com

Design by Robert B. Cumming, Jr.

Library of Congress Cataloging-in-Publication Data

Whisnant, Luke.
Down in the flood : stories / Luke Whisnant.
    p. cm.
ISBN-13: 978-0-916078-69-0 (hardcover : alk. paper)
ISBN-10: 0-916078-69-8 (hardcover : alk. paper)
ISBN-13: 978-0-916078-70-6 (pbk. : alk. paper)
ISBN-10: 0-916078-70-1 (pbk. : alk. paper)
I. Title.
PS3573.H4438D69 2006
813'.54—dc22

                              2006010573

Acknowledgments

The author is grateful to the following publications for permission to reprint:

American Short Fiction: "Boy Poets."
Arts and Letters: "Down in the Flood" and "How to Build a House."
Beloit Fiction Journal: "Selkie."
Emrys Journal: "The Secret University."
Grand Street: "Across from the Motoheads."
The Kennesaw Review: "Three Weddings."
New Mexico Humanities Review: "Wallwork."
The Nebraska Review: "Forgeries."
Neo Revista: "Balm."
The Raleigh News & Observer's Sunday Reader: "Mexican Carwreck."

"How To Build A House" was reprinted in *New Stories from the South: The Year's Best: 2006.*
"Wallwork" was reprinted in *New Stories from the South: The Year's Best: 1986.*
"Across from the Motoheads" was reprinted in *New Stories from the South: The Year's Best: 1987*, and in *This Is Where We Live: Short Stories by 25 Contemporary North Carolina Writers.*
"In the Hurricane" was a finalist in the *Glimmer Train* 2006 Open Fiction Competition.

By water shall he die, and take his end.
—Shakespeare, *Henry VI Pt 2*

If you go down in the flood,
It's gonna be your own fault.
—Dylan, "Down in the Flood"

Contents

Mexican Carwreck

A Ditch

HERE IS WHERE: the slick wet curve off-camber, the blacktop pitted with patches and ruts, the yellow double line faded almost invisible. A ditch along either side; standing water stinking of rot and hot rubber and hogshit; dockweed, mullein, wild onion, a spray of tiny yellow flowers with faces turned up to the rain. Blue styrofoam Fillet of Fish. Rusted barbed wire. Skidmarks like screaming. A body facedown in the ditch. Turn him over.

Bodies

SIX BODIES. ONE in the ditch. Two in the tobacco past the ditch. One on the blacktop, one across the curve with his head crushed against a fence post, one so far flung that he isn't found for a quarter-hour, and then only because a small brown dog circles him, whimpering. Six bodies. Every single one of them thrown from the vehicle. It's a cultural thing, the sheriff says for TV; they won't wear their seatbelts. Seatbelts are not macho. And of course there's never no kind of excuse for riding in the back like that.

State troopers with a yellow measuring tape, marking points of impact. The *wump-skreet, wump-skreet* of windshield wipers on an idle ambulance. An EMT strapping up a sheet-wrapped stretcher, weeping.

A Witness

NAME'S HERBERT JOSLYN. I live up here about a quarter mile. I was the first on the scene. Just awful. I was in Korea, and saw nothing worst. A head-on Mexican carwreck. These fellas lived right up the road and was good neighbors, even if they couldn't speak much English. It's their families I feel sorry for.

The state has turned its back on this road. This curve was never engineered right from Day One, nor maintained either. Five times now I've complained, and twice they've had their engineers out here, but you see what all good that done. Hell, yes, you can quote me, but no photographs. I got a microchip in me that breaks cameras. You think I'm foolin but I'm not.

Clothing

GOODWILL BLUEJEANS A size too big or too small. Used teeshirts, discolored under the arms, or frayed doubleknits in lurid colors. Greasy adjust-a-band baseball caps: grinning Indians, leaping Marlins. Holes in old gray socks. But the shoes are new, new Nikes, all six pairs, black or blue uppers with neon green trim, see-through soles with magic air pockets. So you can fly.

Not Mexico

IT'S JUST SUCH a damn stereotype, you know? one of the cops says: Mexicans crammed into the back of a pickup truck. You just cringe when you see it. It's like white people wearing bermuda shorts and pennyloafers, or black people eating watermelon.

Watermelon, cucumbers, strawberries. Tobacco here, peaches in South Carolina. Tomatoes in Georgia. Back here late summer for the tobacco harvest. In-between times, roofing or landscaping.

Living in a 30-year-old mobile home up on cinderblocks, three to a room. Sending what they can back home to Guatemala and Honduras. Not Mexico.

The Other Driver

NONE OF THE dead has ID. That's one rumor. All of the dead have ID, but names won't be released until next of kin are notified. That's another rumor. The cops run a license check on the red truck and find the plate was stolen. They check the VIN. Nobody seems to know anything. The TV camera guys are sweating under clear plastic ponchos. The reporters touch up their lipstick, then do their standups. Someone says on camera that this is the worst wreck in county history. Someone else says that's bull. The cops tell the media people to take a hike, to clear out and let them do their jobs. The media people say they have a job to do too, give them a break, they're on deadline. One or another of them shake their heads, disgusted. Cops vs. reporters: it's a little dance they could do in their sleep.

The other driver sits in the rain on the running board of his dump truck, head in hands. The raindrops on his face make it hard to tell if he's crying. They slid into my lane, he says over and over. I stood on the brakes but couldn't get it stopped. I wasn't going any faster than fifty, I swear to God. —The TV people, shooed away by sheriff's deputies, scatter and stand aside a moment, then nonchalantly regroup around the dump truck, shooting surreptitiously from the hip.

Thrown Clear

IN THEIR POCKETS: a CP&L electric bill for $58.73 stamped PAID. Cheap Food Lion sunglasses. Camels in crush-proof packs, crushed. Twenty dollar bills, five dollar bills, wads of ones, loose change, two Mexican pesos, a Honduran 50-centavo. A plastic toothpick dispenser. A roll of breath mints. A silver and turquoise ring. A three-pack of condoms, ribbed, and another three-pack, lubricated. A pocket watch with the crystal smashed.

Thrown clear: an English-Spanish phrasebook. A requinto, a four-string guitar shaped from an armadillo shell. Five loads of dirty laundry in black milkcrates. A black tarp the size of a pickup bed. The limping brown dog scuffling and whimpering around the ambulances.

Reverse

THE MOMENT OF death hovers over the dead: weightless, a song no one hears, the moment of death and the moment before. It doesn't matter who believes this. It's true. Here, at the edge of a field a thousand miles from home, their moment is hovering. If you could put the truck in reverse, if driving backward were like rewinding a tape, you could enter the moment before: the moment of bliss, absolute and immutable. You could know what it meant to huddle with your compadres under a flapping tarp, tasting the summer drizzle on your face, glad that the rain had given you a day off so you could ride into town and do laundry. You could sing with your best friend the happy words about the banker's dark-haired daughter and the poor country boy, harmonizing over the high thrum of the requinto. You could roar with laughter, helpless, hugging the neck of the man next to you, gasping and weeping tears of joy at the dog—the dog singing along in his mournful howls and yelps, this pathetic wonderful North American singing dog.

And then the moment gone in an instant, the panicked creature sliding and scrambling, skittering with his long toenails across the metal bed of the truck, and everyone shouting as you head into the final curve.

Selkie

SUMMER SHALLCROSS IS her real name, but before the divorce it was the custom in her family to use nicknames—Da for her father, brothers Bonkie and Pepper, mother Mothra after the flying foe of Godzilla—and so she's been known as Selkie since before she could speak. She grew up spelling it as it sounded, and refused to change it upon first encountering the word in print: "selchie" did not look right to her; she tried it on and found it didn't fit. Selkie is twelve years old and (excepting her feet) small for her age, slender, with long limbs gawky and graceful by turns. She has long blonde hair and limpid, wide-set eyes the green-gray color of seawater after a storm. Her skin is fair and very fine, and at certain times, such as the application of sunblock to the small of the back, inspires the name "Silkie"; when she pouts, she is known as "Sulkie." Like the mythical selchie, she too loves the water; she too could be half seal. She would rather read than watch TV, and she'd rather swim than read, but best of all is to read in the tub. For her birthday, her brothers, who live now with their father, bought her bubble bath; her mother's new boyfriend—The Boyfiend, they call him—gave her a copy of *The Hobbit* and a beanie baby stuffed seal.

THE BOYFIEND WATCHES Mothra packing for an all-day rehearsal. Into the plush-lined zip-up gigbag goes the cello: *z-i-i-p*. Her horsehair bow she stores in its own compartment: *z-i-i-p*. She zips into the outer pocket a sheaf of sheet music, a foil-wrapped sandwich, a tin of aspirin. "Thanks for taking care of her," she says.

"It'll be fun," the Boyfiend says. "We'll catch the new Jackie Chan."

"You're funny. She's been wanting to go to the art museum. That should kill an hour or so."

"You're sure its open Sundays?"

"All art museums are open Sundays. Goof." The Mothra kisses him sweetly. "Selkie's been on this Pre-Raphaelite kick lately. Fairy queens and mermaids and naiads and nymphs—all those naked waifs with their little boobies. She's going through a little boobie stage."

One of the Boyfiend's better qualities is empathy in the area of feminine physiology; for example, once a month, without being reminded, he brings Mothra a box of medicinal chocolate. But Selkie's breast fixation elicits from him only a guarded *Hmm*.

Off goes the Mothra to her all-day rehearsal; into the Boyfiend's Subaru go the damp-haired waif, just out of her bath, and her babysitter, though he is careful not to use that term, for fear of incurring the Selkie's ire. Instead he revs the engine and cranks the radio, looking at her quizzically.

She picks up her cue. With hands over her ears, Selkie, who is ignorant of pop music, even the crooning Jeremy-Jason-Brandon boy-bands her girlfriends swoon for, screams to the Boyfiend, "Is this what Mom calls devil music?"

"Devil music? No!" he screams back. "This is head-banging music!"

"It's really really loud!" she screams.

"Yes!" he screams. "You got to play it loud!"

"Louder than this!"

"Yes!"

"How loud!"

"Until the speakers rattle!"

So she reaches over and cranks it further, until the speakers *do* rattle, and he teaches her the song's refrain, and how to bang her head, and the little Subaru rocks and bounces as they stab and slash at their air guitars and scream of being on the Highway to Hell, yeah, the Highway to Hell, yeah yeah, though actually they haven't yet left the driveway.

SHE WANTS TO go to the art museum not, as she says, for any Pre-Raphaelite bunk, but because there's a student show up, paintings by some of the kids in her school. So they go.

The sign in the foyer reads "Imitations and Intimations: Masterpieces from the County Schools. May 3-24, Second Floor." Up the oaken stairs the Selkie clomps in her size-seven sandals. The Boyfiend, tagging after, asks if she has anything in the show.

"Mine wasn't good enough," she says, shrugging one shoulder.

The idea, she explains, was to take a famous painting, like by a famous artist or something, and copy it, but not copy it exactly, like you know, maybe change the colors or the faces or something like that.

Sure enough, they find the upstairs gallery crammed wall-to-wall with kid knockoffs of Mona Lisas, American Gothics, Washingtons Crossing the Delaware, even some Op Art and a few Pollocks that could fool almost anyone.

Selkie zigzags a bit, then bee-lines to a Picasso copy, *El Viejo Guitarista*, a blue-and-gray study of an old man cradling a guitar. She tilts her head left, then right, then left again, squints, takes two steps back. "Huh," she says. "It looks like he's laying down. How could you lay down and play a guitar?" The Boyfiend says that Jimi Hendrix was famous for lying down and playing guitar, but this means nothing to Selkie. "It's not right. It's supposed to be like this"— she waves her hand up and down—"but they hung it like this. It's upside down. I mean, not upside down, sideways."

"Oriented wrong," the Boyfiend offers. "They've got it landscape and it should be portrait."

"Whatever."

"You're sure?"

"Of course I'm sure," Selkie says disdainfully.

"How do you know?"

"I just know. Because we saw the original painting in the class and it was like up and down. And because I know the boy that painted it. He sits across from me in Art."

Joey Kalinowski, the typed card on the wall reads, *B.R. Barnes Middle School. The Old Guitarist, Pablo Picasso.*

"I've never heard you mention any Joey," the Boyfiend says.

"Yeah, well." Again the one-shouldered shrug.

"Well, let's see if Allison can fix this for us."

"Who's Allison?"

Allison is the assistant to the associate director of the museum, and she's downstairs updating the website when they knock. Without introducing Selkie, the Boyfiend explains the problem. "Of course you're right—the original Picasso is vertically oriented," Allison says. "The technicians hanging the kid show must not have realized that. I'll take care of it right away. Very observant little girl you've got here, James. Beautiful, too. She's like a little fairy-child, isn't she? Dreamy and a bit ephemeral." The Selkie feigns indifference. The Boyfiend compliments Allison's new perm.

"For all the good it does me," she says bitterly.

Back in the car, the Boyfiend helps Selkie adjust her seatbelt. "Dreamy and a bit ephemeral," he says sarcastically. Selkie wants to know what *that* was all about. "Allison used to be my girlfriend," the Boyfiend explains. "We broke up because she wanted to get married and have babies, and I didn't. At least not with her."

"Huh," Selkie says.

"This was years ago, you understand."

"Uh huh." She puts both feet on the dash. "So you used to kiss her and stuff?"

The Boyfiend laughs so hard he nearly runs a red light. He coughs and chokes and laughs some more. Finally he is able to say that Yes, he used to kiss her and stuff. "Huh," Selkie says again. She stares out her window. After a moment the Boyfiend informs her, teasingly, that a Joey is a baby kangaroo.

"Nuh nah!" Selkie says. She's blushing; she starts to giggle.

At Bombay Tandoor on Monday evening, Mothra puts down her fork and announces, "Bar none, this is the worst Indian restaurant I have ever eaten in."

A slight pause. Then the scowling Boyfiend agrees darkly, saying that in fact it does not qualify as a restaurant at all: "It's more of a Hindoo Coin-Laundry Vomitorium."

Usually the Boyfiend tries to time such utterances to coincide with Mothra's sippage of water, in hopes of causing it to come out her nose. In this instance he is successful.

"You are quite insane," Mothra tells him when she has recovered. "Pay him no mind, Selkie. He's filling your head with rubbish."

The Selkie does pay him no mind; using the back of her spoon, she is busy methodically coating with tamarind sauce both sides of each piece of her usual Chicken Pakora. When she achieves the proper level of saturation, she begins to eat, ignoring the Boyfiend's lament that her palate lacks adventurousness and that she may as well be eating Chicken McNuggets; he insists that next time she must try something different, the Cat Pakora, say, or the Hamster Vindaloo. The Selkie barely pauses to roll her eyes. She gobbles down her soggy pakoras, picks at a bit of rice, turns up her nose at the raita, guzzles another Coke. Eventually she pushes away her plate, sated. She slouches, then puts both elbows on the table, cradles her chin, and wrinkles her nose at the Boyfiend. He wrinkles his back. She ties her napkin into a tight knot, teases the long ends up like ears, and begins hopping it across the table. "I'm a bunny rabbit," she says. "I'm a bunny rabbit." The Boyfiend, setting aside his lukewarm Aloo Gobhi, takes up his yellow napkin and ties it similarly, but with smaller ears, like those on a Doberman. "I'm a Pokémon," he growls. "I'm Pikachu. I hate bunny rabbits." "Eeek," the Selkie's bunny rabbit says, "Pokémons suck." "Don't say suck," Mothra tells her. "Yes, don't say suck," the Boyfiend says, "say bite." "Pokémons bite," Selkie says. Boyfriend: "I will bite *you*, little rabbit." The Pokémon and the rabbit wrestle across the blue batik tablecloth.

On their way to the car, the Selkie explains in her own inimitable manner that the food is insipid and the service wretched because the family that runs the Bombay Tandoor are Patels, and Patels are hoteliers, not restaurateurs. The Boyfiend begins laughing. "Wherever did you hear such a thing?" Mothra wonders. "At school," the Selkie says, quite huffy; "Angelisa Singh told me, and her daddy told her."

"I suppose he should know," Mothra murmurs, unlocking the car.

"*Her* daddy wears a turban," Selkie explains, looking wistfully at the Boyfiend.

A FEW MINUTES LATER, Selkie, slumped sideways across the backseat, watches the scythe-like moon out the rear window and weeps hot quiet tears as Mothra and the Boyfiend say goodnight (two quick kisses in his condo parking lot). She declines her mother's offer of the now-vacant front seat, then begins to sob as soon as they're back on the boulevard. What is it, what is it? For a half-dozen redlights she won't say, but finally wails a few broken phrases, and—

"Summer, *what* are you talking about?" Mothra says. "Stop crying; I can't understand a word you're saying."

She has forgotten a homework assignment. She has totally forgotten to do it, and now it's too late, and tomorrow it's International Day and when the other kids come in with their Flags of Nations, she'll be the only kid without a Flag of Nation, and everyone will laugh at her, everyone, and Ms. McManus will give her a big red zero and put it on the bulletin board beside her name where everyone can see it, she can't possibly go to school tomorrow, please don't make me go without my Flag of Nation, please?

Now Mothra drives with one hand reaching behind her, stroking her Selkie's tear-streaked face. She makes a kissing sound. She coos and reassures. She says for Selkie not to worry, never worry: has she forgotten the secret stock of posterboard that Mothra keeps for just such an emergency? the magic marker drawer? the hot glue gun? "And I happen to know," Mothra says, "yes indeed I do, that there is a page on the Internet, maybe even a dozen such pages, devoted entirely to Flags of All Nations."

"But—" the Selkie sobs.

"Hush, hush," Mothra says lovingly. "We can fix it. Let me fix it for you."

This is why Selkie will tell anyone that she has the Best Mothra in All the World.

At home they brew cups of thick cocoa, crank up the computer, and slip off their shoes. "Why El Salvador?" Selkie says, staring into the monitor.

"Trust me," Mothra tells her. "It's simple, and therefore quick, and in this instance, time is of the essence. Baby blue here and here, posterboard white there, *voila!*"

Selkie uncaps a blue marker, bends over a piece of posterboard. She begins filling in with quick tiny strokes in a trembling hand. "Are you guys going to get married?" she asks suddenly.

"Would you like that?"

"I dunno. Maybe."

"I tell you what. If we start talking about it, we'll ask you first. We'll be sure to include you in the decision-making process."

"Huh. You didn't ask me when you married Daddy."

"Well, duh, Selkie."

"Because I wasn't born. I know. But you didn't ask me when you divorced Daddy, either."

"We've gone over this again and again."

"Because, listen, when you and Daddy were still—"

It is almost midnight before they finish the flag of El Salvador.

Over supper the next night the Boyfiend is treated to a detailed re-enactment of the episode, with Mothra doing Selkie's lines (falsetto) and Selkie doing Mothra and Ms. McManus (alto). Then Selkie stands, bows, and into the make-believe mic of her fist begins to sing, to the tune of "Christmas Tree, O Christmas Tree," a lyric she wrote that morning in homeroom:

> *O Salvador, O Salvador,*
> *You really are not such a bore.*
> *Your flag is fine, I must confess*
> *And helped me out of the homework mess.*
> *O Salvador! O! O! O! O!*

The Boyfiend claps and cheers, and asks to see the posterboard flag. It's at school, he is informed; all the flags are on display at school. He asks her to describe it. She does. He says there must be some mistake, that he thought the Salvadoran flag depicted an eagle eating a snake. "That's the Mexican flag!" Selkie says. "You are misinformed," Boyfiend tells her; "the Mexican flag shows an armadillo eating a lizard." Selkie laughs hysterically, then says with as much disdain as she can muster, "Nuh nah." They get silly; they vie for the funniest nature scene. On the Madagascar flag: a lemur eating a luna moth. Tanzania: an elephant eating a peanut. Japan: Godzilla eating Mothra ("Watch it," Mothra warns). Australia: "A wombat," the Boyfiend says, pausing dramatically, "eating a joey."

Mothra wants to know what's so funny, why Selkie is blushing bright red and can't stop giggling.

AFTER INTERNATIONAL DAY comes Rock Star Day, for which the school suspends what the Boyfiend calls their crypto-fascist dress code: on this day and this day only, girls may show bare shoulders and belly buttons. Selkie does, with a vengeance, in a purple crop-top not much bigger than a jog-bra. She and three cronies tart themselves up as Spice Girls, though Selkie claims to have never knowingly heard a Spice Girl song; it's just an excuse to run hog-wild through Mothra's makeup drawer, dump glitter in her hair, and dress in Salvation Army velvet hiphuggers and Mothra's four-inch Putenesca Platforms, which are only a half-size too big, and which she leaves on after school and well into the evening. "I'm taller than you are," she sing-songs before supper, patting her mother's head and calling her "My Little Mothra." "Cover your navel," Mothra says in mock-horror, snapping a dish-towel at her. Selkie sways and staggers into the den, dodging the cello, dancing, swinging her little hips, both hands hiding her tummy, and crashes onto the saggy sofa beside the Boyfiend, who peers at her through laced fingers. "I can't look," he explains, looking anyway; the flirty Selkie winks at him.

"One of y'all set the table," Mothra calls.

"I can't set the table," Selkie says.

"Why not?"

"I'm too busy covering my navel."

"I sigh at you," Mothra tells her, then does so. The Boyfiend heads for the silverware drawer. "Who were some of the other kids dressed as?" he asks.

Well, Selkie explains, there were lots of kids dressed as rappers, you know, hip-hop. And lots of kids that just dressed funny and you couldn't really tell who they were. And Naomi was this, like, punk rocker. And Brandon and some other guy were both Elvis, two Elvises. And Joey was Bob Marlow. "Bob Marlow?" the Boyfiend says, "who is that?"

Selkie huffs and puts her fists on her hips, indignant. "*You* know! Bob Marlow. He, like, had his hair in dreads and like a tie-dye teeshirt. And he called everybody *mon*."

"Oh," the Boyfiend says, "*that* Bob Marlow."

During supper, for no apparent reason, a kind of lethargy seems to come over Selkie; sighing, she slides into one of her dreaded monosyllabic sulks ("no," "huh," "kay," "um"), punctuated once by the much-despised "whatever." She picks mournfully at her mac-&-cheese, normally one of her favorites, as Mothra and Boyfiend deconstruct their days and play footsie under the table ("You guys are kicking me," she whines). In a listless funk she dumps her dish into the sink, says she thinks she'll brush toofs and head to bed.

"It's not even eight o'clock," the Boyfiend points out when she has gone.

"She had a big day," Mothra says. "And tomorrow is Crazy-Backwards Day. Will this week never end?"

"Still," the Boyfiend says. "What's up with her? She's so moody lately."

"She's twelve. Weren't you ever twelve?"

They hold hands across the pale green glass-top table, watching down the hall for the light under Selkie's door to go out.

SELKIE DOES NOT attend Crazy-Backwards Day, a day when students wear their clothes inside-out or underwear-on-top and are served upside-down cake for lunch, when custodians teach classes and teachers sweep the halls, when first period comes last, and vice versa. Selkie doesn't attend because she wakes up ill, feeling cramped and sick to her stomach, feeling, she says, the worst she can ever remember feeling. Mothra lets her go back to sleep, and later, by request, braids her hair in pigtails, a style Selkie has not worn since she was a little girl. They eat tomato soup and saltines and then go shopping, some things they need, some things they want: lightbulbs, aspirin, pony-print cotton socks, Mars bars, purple plastic coat hangers, a coloring book and crayons, Mydol, a bright blue bowl just because it was so pretty.

They spend the day together and (after a quick explanatory phone call) take the night off from the Boyfiend. At bedtime,

Selkie folds herself up into her mother's lap, buries her face in her neck, and sobs. "I don't want them to come this weekend," she says through her tears. "Who?" Mothra says. "Pepper and Bonkie. I hate them." "Oh, Selkie. Of course you don't hate them. You love them." "I hate them," Selkie says, and then begins listing the other people she hates: her father, Ms. McManus, Angelisa Singh, the Boyfiend. "Stop, now," Mothra says; "you're being silly." She kisses her daughter's damp forehead, squeezes her tight. "I hate everything and everybody," Selkie says, crying harder. "I don't want to go to Bingo Night. I didn't want this to happen. I want to be a little girl. I don't want to grow up. I hate growing up. I want to stay your baby. I want to be a baby again."

And then the Boyfiend, unexpected, is at the door, bearing a single red rose for his belovéd and a bar of Godiva dark chocolate with raspberry for his Selkie. "For medicinal purposes," he says sympathetically.

Embarrassed, the teary Selkie tears open the wrapper and thrusts the candy into her mouth. By the time Mothra and the Boyfiend have found a bud vase and filled it with water, the chocolate is gone.

BINGO NIGHT, THE last event of School Spirit Week, is held in the cafeteria, a bland institutional expanse made more melancholy by desperate touches of bulletin-board color. Going in, the Boyfiend, who buys three cards each for Selkie and Mothra but only one for himself, says it's no use, everybody else might as well hang it up, because he is the five-time world champion of Bingo. "Nuh nah," Selkie says, but her mind seems elsewhere. She scopes the crowd, first feigning disinterest, then furtively. Mothra, watching closely, asks Selkie where she'd like to sit. Selkie shrugs.

They find a spot up front, near the prize table, a long clutter of donated junk, and Selkie insists on saving a seat—for whom, she won't say. "Winning card picks a prize," screams the lady gym-teacher; there's no P.A. She begins bellowing the numbers: "Bee! Twelve! Bee! Twelve!" "I wouldn't be twelve again if you paid me," Mothra says, deadpan, but Selkie cracks nary a smile. The smirking Boyfiend wins the second game.

"How in the heck did he do that?" Mothra says.

The Boyfiend gets his card validated and then is turned loose on the prize table. "C'mon, Selkie," he says, "help me pick somethin'." They paw through Greatest Hits CDs, scented candles, pen-&-pencil sets, glow-in-the-dark whistling yo-yos. Selkie holds up one odd thing after another, being ironic. "How about this useful package of clarinet reeds?" she suggests.

Finally the Boyfiend snags a road emergency kit—flares, a multi-tool, a space blanket—for Mothra's car.

"So romantic," Mothra says, kissing him.

Selkie, standing, scans the room. She starts to wave at someone, then stops, looking crestfallen and uncertain. Joey has just arrived. A lanky boy in a red teeshirt, he's flanked on the left by an exotically turbaned man and on the right by an exotically pretty girl—a girl whose skin is the color of masala tea, a girl with whom he's holding hands.

"So that's Joey," Mothra observes; like all good Mothras she has intuition from hell and eyes in the back of her head. She glances at Selkie's saved seat. "Shall we invite him to sit with us?"

"Don't you dare," Selkie hisses. She slumps down in her chair and stares at her hands.

Ten minutes later, the Boyfiend, rising to his feet, calls out another Bingo. "Lucky card," he explains to the skeptics at their table. This time he earns his kiss by bagging a big bromeliad with pink blossoms, passing up his heart's desire, the North Korean All-N-1 Socket Wench. "Are you cheating, Mr. Shallcross?" a kid at their table asks him. The Boyfiend smiles and squeezes Mothra's hand. "Hey, Summer, is your dad cheating?" the kid asks Selkie. "He's not my dad," Selkie says, annoyed.

For the next hour no one at their table wins. Selkie, neglecting her cards, makes frequent sorties through the cafeteria, ostensibly for the water fountain or restroom or to say hi to friends; she slips from group to group, conducting whispered conferences and hailing allies over the screaming gym teacher. She gives the Singh table a wide berth, although some of her coterie reconnoiter and report back. "I know I'm being dense," the Boyfiend says, watching them between games, "but is something going on?"

"Yes," Mothra says.

Selkie returns to the table. "Can we go home now?"

"Sit down," Mothra says; "they're almost out of prizes. Maybe you'll win one yet."

"No I won't," Selkie says despondently.

"You don't know that, sweetie."

"Yes I do."

The Boyfiend hands her his two-time winner. "It's a lucky card," he tells Selkie. "Here, you play it."

She does play it, desultorily, and is as astonished as anyone when she wins the very next game.

"They're going to have to retire that card," Mothra says, shaking her head and laughing.

It's slim pickins at the prize table after a full night of Bingo; Selkie paces up and down its length thrice, then beckons the Boyfiend. "Help me," she says. "If you were a boy, what prize would you pick?"

Of course the Boyfiend *is* a boy, but he refrains from any smart-assed commentary. They consider a string of blinking white Christmas lights, a flashlight-keychain combo, a book of Pizza Shack gift certificates, a carved kudu left over from Kwanzaa. Selkie shakes her head before a red-and-blue Siamese fighting fish floating belly-up in a small glass bowl. There are no stuffed kangaroos, she observes morosely. At last the Boyfiend finds a set of ruby-handled mini-screwdrivers hidden under a plaid throw-pillow. "How about this?" he says. "Every good boy deserves screwdrivers."

The Selkie snatches the package, waves it at the Assistant Principal Prize Monitor, and checks it off on his list. But when she wheels toward the tables, she sees that Joey and the Singhs are gone.

"*Damn* it!" Selkie cries, stomping her foot.

This is the first time Mothra and the Boyfiend have ever heard her curse.

ON THE DARK ride home, they're mostly quiet, listening to a tape of Mothra's most recent rehearsal. "Put on your seatbelt, Selkie," Mothra says after a few minutes.

"Okay," Selkie says, but she doesn't. Instead she sprawls supine across the car's back seat, craning her neck to peer out the rear window. "What *are* you doing?" her mother wants to know. "Looking for the moon," she says. "I think the moon has already set," the Boyfiend tells her. "Well *I* can still see it," Selkie murmurs. Mothra glances in her mirror; the Boyfiend turns around in his seat to look. Through the translucent red of a screwdriver handle, their Selkie squints skyward.

Across from the Motoheads

THEY'RE AT IT again. From Gran's screened-in porch we can see straight into their front yard, where amongst corroded junk and clumps of weeds a Harley hangs, chained ten feet up to an old oak branch. Rust-pitted, skeletal, like some strange carcass swinging dry in the wind, it's their banner, their heraldic arms: here live the Motoheads. They stand outside in full view, large and hairy, troglodyte, popping beers and burning red meat over an open-pit fire—a brick-lined hole dug with much cursing in the early afternoon. Their chests are bare under sleeveless jeans jackets. They roar at each other not to park their bikes on the lawn. They park their bikes on the lawn.

Gran says she's not afraid of dopers and that she's seen them worse. We believe her. Like everywhere else, the neighborhood has gone downhill. Even the cops lock their car doors. "They ain't gonna do a thing to me but maybe burn my house down with me inside it," Gran says. She won't move, though. She's lived here for twenty-two years, ever since she got back from Manila. "I wish you could have seen the yards there—pretty as a golf course. And every blade in place. You can't get help like that here, I hope to tell you. Those Filipinos. They cut the grass with a scissors, one piece at a time, down on their knees."

My uncle Bubba laughs because he's heard all this so many times before and because Gran's been after him for two days now to mow the lawn. But Pop's old push mower's too dull to cut, he says; it just smashes the grass flat.

Gran snorts. "Looks like my own son could do some yard work

once in a while instead of me paying good money to those little black boys," she says. "What do you think, Jake?"

"Pretty damn slack," I say, winking at Bubba.

We've been looking at TV. Most nights Gran does up the supper dishes, I put the food away while Bubba sits; then we watch the news. It's still too hot to stay inside, though, and so we move out to the porch as soon as we can. Bubba and my mother bought Gran an air conditioner last summer, but she doesn't like to run it much; "Gives me the arthritis," she says. Tonight Newsroom Five from Charlotte showed a segment about a handgun crackdown, and that reminded Gran of something: she herself had once bought a gun, without a license.

It's been a while since I've heard her tell it, so I ask. And Bubba shakes his head, laughing.

"You can laugh now," Gran says. "I don't remember as you laughed then."

He hadn't been in Korea a week, she says, speaking directly to me and ignoring him, before a letter came: Dear Mom, sell anything you got, get me a .38 and send it airmail. All the guys say if your rifle jams, and the gooks are charging... Gran shivered just to think of it, she says. "I went out that afternoon and sold our radio—and it was brand new, a new Philco, I think—and where I sold it they showed me two little guns, I don't remember what kind now, and so I got one, the biggest one, and with bullets too, because who could say if Bubba could of got the kind he needed there in Korea. And it burnt a hole in my bag all the way back on the streetcar; the conductor was looking at me funny, asked me was I okay, and all the people were looking at me like they could see through my clothes. All those men.... When I got that gun home I closed all the drapes and put it dead center of the kitchen table and then I set down and just looked at it. I was shaking like a pudding."

"Where was Pop?" Bubba says.

"He wasn't here."

She bought a big fruitcake. She hollowed it out and set the gun inside and wrapped the whole thing in wax paper and then in newspaper, in the *Weekly Gazette* social page with a photo of one of Bubba's prom dates announcing her engagement—"

"Which I never even noticed and never heard you say nothing about till now," says Bubba—

"—and yes it was, don't contradict me, Ellen Louise that married what's-his-name, you know the one I mean, divorced just a few years ago and never did have a single child."

"Maybe I ought to look her up," Bubba says. Gran tells him he's broken enough poor girls' hearts in this town, and Bubba just blows her a kiss off the ends of his fingers. I forgot to mention that he separated from his second wife two weeks ago and has been up here from north Florida eating Gran's home cooking ever since and lying around in his T-shirt and army fatigues full of holes like they'd been hit with buckshot or like he'd spilled battery acid on them.

Across the street the Motoheads are dancing weird sixties dances and laughing at themselves. Their arms make swimming motions in the air, their torsos bend and jerk, their heavy feet hardly move. Two shaggy Moto women dance with each other. They toss their heads like dirty horses.

"What happened to the gun?" I ask.

"You know what happened to it," Bubba says.

She sent it to Korea. She stood in line at the post office and hefted it in her hands and wondered how to stop her voice from shaking. And she told the counter clerk it was a fruitcake.

"I was sick for months about that thing. I thought that I had bought something for my only boy to help him kill somebody and it like to made me crazy. I couldn't stop thinking about it nights, couldn't sleep, couldn't eat, 'cause here was Bubba off in that Godawful faraway place and maybe he was shooting at people with a gun I had bought. I don't know why the army don't give enough guns to its soldiers, you'd think they would, wouldn't you?

But he just had to have it, and so I went out and broke every law in America for that gun, and it got so I couldn't pass a *police* on the corner without ducking my head. Every night I prayed. And for a solid year I hid whenever the mailman come to the door."

And Bubba laughs and laughs and says, "She was afraid they were gonna return to sender, and she'd have to find something to do with it, find some way to get rid of the damn thing."

"I worried about it every blesséd minute till Bubba come home from that awful place. And he didn't have a single gun on him. Not his rifle or even a bayo-net or the pistol or anything. Just his uniform, khakis, they called them. And do you know what he had the nerve to tell me about that pistol," Gran says, "that I had broken every law in America for and could go to jail for and maybe even the electric chair?"

"No," I lie.

"Lost it in a poker game," Bubba says.

GRAN SAYS HE had to go to Korea to stay out of trouble. And Bubba, gray-haired, grinning, laughs.

"You laugh," he tells me, "can't nothing touch you. That's all I learnt over there."

It's early still. The sidewalk puddles are still pink from holding the sun all day. A kid at the stop sign burns rubber, the Motoheads cheer derisively, and I know that the story I've heard ten thousand times, as regular as moonrise, is coming up again:

"Most everybody'd pulled back," Bubba says, "running like bejesus—"

But he was cut off. He knew to run south, since they were fighting the *North* Koreans, but somehow he'd gotten turned around in a snowstorm. Hugging the ground, circling back through a scree-clotted valley, he'd lost his wits and his rifle and he almost ran smack into a tank. He stood there, muzzle to muzzle, you might say, and the turret swung and stopped and lowered itself and drew a bead on his heart, two feet away, and Bubba laughed. He could smell the barrel—powder, oil, and heat rising off it in waves—and he could have reached out and touched it—that's how close he was. Fish or cut bait, you slanteyed sons of bitches, Bubba *says* he said, and then he sat down in the snow and laughed.

Probably inside the tank the Chinese were laughing too, since there wasn't anything else they could do. Something about my uncle appealed to them, I guess, sitting cross-legged there, scratching himself and grinning, or maybe they just couldn't see such a waste of heavy ordnance, overkill, blowing a hole the size of a football into a man at such close range, blood and tissue flying everywhere. Maybe somebody made a joke about how it would ruin the shine on their brand-new nice clean tank, and then they got tickled and couldn't machine-gun him.

He walked away. Inside of half a minute the blizzard had covered him from view and he came to his senses and began to run. For the rest of the war he tried not to shoot anyone unless he had to. "I even gave Gran's gun away," he says, "lost it in that poker game."

What I say is what I always say: "That's a good story, Bubba."

The phone rings and Gran comes back a minute later to tell Bubba that his mother-in-law wants to talk with him. "There sure is no love lost between the two of you," Bubba says, rolling out of the hammock and heading indoors.

"Well, she's been calling every blesséd night," Gran tells me. "Set your clock by it. I don't know what's wrong with that boy, Jake, that he'd leave Bonnie. She's just as sweet to him as she can be."

"Maybe he's just restless."

"Huh. Just no account, you mean."

I ask if Bubba really used to be wild.

"Lord, yes. Hot rodding up and down the street, running with a fast crowd, drinking. I don't guess they had all these drugs back then, but he'd of done 'em if they had. Pop had to bail him out of jail one time too many, and finally the judge said Bubba could join the army, or else get sent up to the penitentiary."

When Bubba comes back out, his face is set like maybe he's decided something. He takes his time reloading himself into the hammock. Gran won't look at him. "Well?" I ask finally.

"Same as yesterday. Had I called Bonnie? Had Bonnie called me? Could she give Bonnie a message from me? 'I wish you two would kiss and make up, I'm so upset, I just don't understand it.' Etcetera, etcetera."

"What did you tell her?"

"I told her I was tired."

Gran makes a disgusted little sound under her breath.

Across the street a Motohead pisses into the fire. Two Motoheads crawl on all fours, barking like dogs. A cop car pulls up, blue light flashing, and then two more. "Look at that," I say.

The cops are all out of their cars and most of them start walking up through the yard, slow and real steady. One Motohead raises his empty hands above his tangled hair. All the other Motoheads raise their hands, grinning. "Hello, officers," they chant. The cops leave their guns sheathed. The 'heads ask them in.

"Looks like a powwow," Bubba says. "Gran, why don't you go in the kitchen and get this boy and me a Co-Cola?"

"I'm not your Gran," she says.

Down in the Flood

1

No one we knew was killed by wind. That in itself seems a wonder, since for five or six howling hours the wind felt almost solid, a thing of physical and deadly substance. An eighty- to ninety-mile-an-hour wind, with gusts up to one-ten—it blows the breath from your body, it crashes and pushes against the side of your house like monster surf. Carried in such a wind were all manner of objects suited to dismemberment, decapitation: shards of plate glass, aluminum highway signs, sheets of galvanized roofing, tree limbs sharp as spears. In town a thousand trees went down; they stabbed through roofs, crushed cars, cut power lines; an airborne oak branch skewered the cupola of the courthouse. On television we watched the 100-year-old steeple of the First Baptist Church, which had survived Hazel and Fran and a half-dozen hurricanes from the days before names, sheer off and shatter into the intersection below, where it lay across Third and Elm like some giant kid's tossed-aside toy.

But no one in our county was killed by wind. We hid, we stayed off the streets, even the cops and fire-fighters, and when the wind blew itself out and the sky cleared and we again opened our doors and windows, waved at our neighbors, walked the disheveled streets, we thought we'd gotten off lucky. That wasn't so bad, we said; but few of us knew then to watch the water. "Hide from wind, run from water," Claudine says, "everybody knows that. We hid fine. But some of us ran the wrong way."

2

WEARING A PAIR of my blue flannel boxers, Claudine sits at my Mac writing email to Lloyd, explaining, I assume, where she is and how she came to be here, writing email because none of her phone calls has made it through.

"If his phone is out, he can't access his email," I remind her.

She keeps typing. The house shudders as a low helicopter floats over, headed for the high school.

During the storm we had fourteen-and-a-half inches of rain in a little over twenty-four hours. Before the storm it had rained for fifteen of the previous nineteen days. In three weeks, then, we had accumulated not quite 26 inches of rainfall—over half our annual average. Two nights after the storm, the river, still rising, was sixteen feet above flood stage. Flood stage is thirteen feet.

At sixteen feet above floodstage, our airport, built on drained wetlands, became a lake. The terminal flooded. Every inch of runway was submerged. Pipers and Cessnas and a Lear Jet belonging to the phosphate plant CEO floated off their chocks and bumped and bounced into and off of each other like rubber ducks in a bathtub.

At sixteen feet, the sandbag retaining wall around the Utilities Commission's main substation gave way, and they powered down before the transformers could go under. The entire county went off the grid and under curfew. We stood on our decks and dry driveways in the perfect darkness, gazing into the most brilliant night sky we had seen in years.

At sixteen feet, they closed the bridges. We have three bridges here. The two new ones, concrete and asphalt, lie low over the river, and they flooded. The third is an old-style steel-and-cable arch, and it stayed dry, just barely, but the approach ramp on the north side flooded, so they closed it too.

Which was how Claudine got stranded on my side of town. She had dropped by to return some of my things—a couple of Dylan

CDs, a nonstick wok, a bottle of jojoba massage oil I'd left at her house once—and I convinced her to stay for supper. It was the first meal we'd shared since the breakup, and we portaged the awkward passages pretty well, I thought. At the door she'd kissed my cheek, told me to take care. Two hours later, after the blackout, she was back, despondent and frightened, asking me to take her in. The state patrol had turned her away at every bridge; every highway and backroad she could reach was flooded. "And then they pulled me over and told me I was breaking curfew. They said at least a half-dozen people had drowned tonight trying to drive through high water." She wouldn't look at me; she looked everywhere but. "I tried for an hour to get Lloyd on my cell phone," she said.

That night in bed she pummeled my chest with both fists and damned me for living on the wrong side of the river.

3

THE POWER IS out for 32 hours, a day and two nights during which Claudine can't call Lloyd because my cordless phones are dead. Now and then she pops next door to Darren's house, where there's a plug-in phone, but *We're sorry, all circuits are busy now; will you please try your call again later.* I burn out three sets of batteries on a CD Walkman, mostly listening to a Dylan song called "Down in the Flood" on track repeat. When I get bored I hand the headphones to Claudine and she switches over to an A.M. radio station that's carrying TV 6 as a simulcast. We listen in shifts. They describe the aerial video; they read the road closings. Every school in the county is out for the rest of the week. "Welcome to Fall Break," I tell Claudine. The Montessori school where she teaches is flooded; the high school where I teach is being used as a homeless shelter. Claudine calls the anchorwoman a "bimbo" for mispronouncing Montessori. "She's new," I say, "cut her some slack." "I know her fiancée," Claudine says. "She's dumb as ditchwater." "For those of you watching us on the radio," the bimbo says; and over the next four days, she says it more than once.

Claudine sits me down to explain that she's with Lloyd now, that just because of last night's momentary lapse in judgment I shouldn't get my hopes up. I remind her that by nature I'm a hopeful kind of guy. "It doesn't mean anything," she says, stroking my cheek; "I just want you to understand that." I tell her that if it doesn't mean anything, then what's the harm in doing it again, but this time with a little more tenderness?

Later, I help Darren uncrate his unused Y2K generator and strap it to a red wheelbarrow glazed with rain. We tank it up with gas siphoned from his Bronco, then Darren trundles it from house to house, a mobile power station, running it an hour here, two hours there, just long enough to heat some water or re-freeze the icebox, long enough to watch a few minutes of TV news. Right neighborly of you, people tell him.

4

WHEN THE POWER comes back on—with a sudden lurch like an old truck starting up, and audible cheers from houses all down the block—we begin to get the TV versions of our eleven flood deaths.

A woman trying to coax her SUV across a flooded creek is swept away, presumed drowned.

A brother and sister playing in their flooded backyard are electrocuted by a downed powerline.

A family of migrant workers, none of whom can swim, is trapped by rising water and drowns together when their mobile home floats off its cinder-block foundation and fills with water.

A man cleaning out his flooded bedroom dies of multiple snakebite wounds when he disturbs a nest of water moccasins.

A boy and his father are drowned trying to rescue some of their cows. Details are sketchy.

And one of the veteran camera operators for Channel 6, videotaping along the edge of the river east of town, is swept away when the muddy bank underfoot suddenly crumbles and he slides, camera, battery pack, and all, into the brown water.

Announcing this last death, the prime-time news anchor, a former theater major who still does Shakespeare In The Park cameos here every summer, quotes with tears in his eyes from one of the *Henry* plays, he can't remember which: "By water shall he die and take his end."

"Ah, God," Claudine says; she's crying too. I take her hand.

The TV people are troupers. Trained to read from teleprompters six-minute news segments, they now work live, no commercials, ad-libbing, reading handwritten bulletins, in eight-hour shifts. They announce ad infinitum the business and factory closings, the impassable roads and possible detours, the revised health advisories (boil all water, update your tetanus shots). They grow testy and snappish, they get punchy and silly. Groping for filler, they advise and caution and speculate. Someone calls to complain of their blatant rumor-mongering. This inspires a reactionary backlash: People call and get patched into the broadcast to say what a fine job the station is doing; people driving by the station drop off burgers, pizzas, flowers. The anchors, shored up by this show of support, spin the phrase "rumor-monger" into subsequent stories, arching ironic eyebrows.

To buy time and fill dead air, they interview anyone who comes by. They do bits with the FEMA agent, the hospital's assistant director of operations, a retired traffic engineer. They bring in the buck-toothed Spanish professor from the community college to translate the latest updates for the Latino community. A maintenance man from a nearby apartment complex drops by to explain how to shut off your power at the fusebox, how to reset your hot water heater, how to test your phone line. It is the first time any of us can remember seeing someone in a tee-shirt behind the anchor desk. A woman from the water plant pleads for us to flush only when necessary: "If it's yellow, let it mellow; if it's brown...." The blonde weekend anchor, the one Claudine calls bimbo, refers to it as "bad water," hunches her shoulders, pushes her stack of papers away, palms face out. Her partner, smirking, pats the back of her hand with two fingers; she half-turns toward him with a panicked smile.

"Check it out!" Darren does a little dance in front of his Magnavox. "What did I tell you?"

"She has a fiancée, Darren," Claudine says. "She's getting married in June. It was in the paper."

"That's yesterday's news, girl," Darren says. "She's doin' this guy. Look at 'em. They're playing footsie under the desk."

Claudine is shaking her head; it's too soap-opera. "No way."

Darren hoots. "Way, Claudine. They're sleeping on cots at the goddamn TV station. What do you expect? Love the one you're with, you know?"

5

EXACTLY HOW LLOYD got my unlisted phone number, I don't know. He is polite, perhaps more than the situation warrants; he identifies himself and says he's looking for Claudine and have I seen her by any chance?

I have seen her, I tell him. In fact, she's here. In fact, she's in the shower just now. I ask if she can call him back.

"I'm at a pay phone," he says, after a five-second pause. "There's maybe twenty people behind me waiting to use this phone." The lines to his neighborhood are still down, he explains.

I offer to take a message.

"I don't think that will be necessary," Lloyd says, and hangs up.

"Suit yourself," I say to the dial tone in my ear.

When I tell Claudine that Lloyd called, she panics. What did I tell him? What did he say? Why in God's name didn't I keep him on the phone another minute, why didn't I come drag her out of the shower, why didn't he leave a message? "He did," I tell her; "he said for you not to bother calling him." She stares at me, wounded, then says she doesn't believe me. I raise one eyebrow, shrug. She snatches at the phone, tries *69 but *we're sorry, the number cannot be accessed by this method, would you please hang up now.* "Bastards," Claudine screeches. She slams the bedroom door and I hear her fling herself across the futon.

A half-hour later she appears in the doorway, wearing jeans and one of my old workshirts, sleeves rolled up. "I've got to get out of here," she says pathetically. "I have to try, or he'll never forgive me. I've run all the gas out of my car. Will you help me?"

"You can't be serious," I say.

"I am. If I have to, I'll ask Darren. I'd rather have you do it, though. Will you help me get back across the river?"

6

WATER SIGNS: BRIDGE OUT. HIGH WATER. DETOUR. ROAD CLOSED. DO NOT ENTER. DANGER. AUGA PELIGROSA.

"Son of a bitch," Claudine says.

My neighborhood is in the bent crook of the river's elbow; the river comes down from the north and dog-legs east a mile from my house. This is geographical fact, I point out to Claudine, and so it stands to reason that every single road leading south or west will be flooded. She insists that we try them anyway. We do. They're flooded—even the four-lane is under water—and the cops have barricaded them to keep fools like us from taking our lives in our hands. Trying to the east, we find the creeks feeding into the river are over their banks too, and have washed out both highways. We go north, thinking that if we can get far enough, we'll be able to jog west and circle back around south of the river, but we're stymied at every turn. "Try this one," Claudine says, pointing at the map in her lap. "Turn here." I do. For eight or ten miles we navigate mostly dry road, swerving around downed trees, until we come to a place where water whirls across the blacktop. I stop the car and hop out.

"It doesn't look all that deep," Claudine says. "And there's dry road on the other side."

She's right. The flooded place is maybe forty or fifty feet wide, and all the way across I can see the double yellow line glowing through the shallow water.

"Let's go for it," she says.

I creep the car into the stream. We make a wake, churning, roiling. Claudine rolls down her window and hangs her head out, watching the level of the water against the tires.

"Piece of cake," she says.

We make it across.

"See?"

I shift up to second, then third. Around the next bend and down a little dip we come upon a huge lake of water across the road, as far as we can see, and deep enough that it's halfway up an S-curve sign. We park and both get out to look and Claudine curses a blue streak, but finally there's nothing to do but turn around and go back.

"Now where?" I ask.

"That's it," she says. "That was the last road on the map."

She folds the map, tosses it into the glovebox, plops her feet on the dashboard, and goes into a funk.

"Look, Claudine," I say after a mile of silence, "we're stuck.

You're just going to have to wait 'til the water goes down. You're going to have to put Lloyd on the back burner for a few days."

"You don't have to act so happy about it."

"I'm not unhappy about it," I admit after a moment. "But this is hard for me, too. I'm getting all these mixed signals."

She rests her cheek on the window and closes her eyes.

"Did he really say not to bother calling him back?"

"He was at a pay phone, Claudine."

"Oh."

After a few more miles she finds a week-old newspaper under her seat and starts reading our horoscopes aloud: hers, Lloyd's, mine.

I point out a SLIPPERY WHEN WET sign, saying it's pretty funny, considering. She doesn't bother to look.

"You know, babe, you and me," she says, putting down the paper, "we were doomed from the start. I'm a Cancer. You're Pisces. A crab and a fish. We're too alike. We're both water signs."

7

DON'T DRINK THE water, don't bathe in the water, don't brush your teeth with the water, don't cut yourself shaving with the water, there are dead animals in the water, there is animal feces and human waste in the water, when going into a house after the water recedes, watch out for snakes. Watch out for every sort of animal, the poor crazed animals, the poor crazed packs of homeless dogs howling at the choppers overhead.

Channel 6 shows video of starving cows trapped inside a mobile home, dead cows floating downriver on their backs, pigs slipping and sliding atop cars and barn tin-roofs, med-evac choppers lifting terrified horses in rescue slings. Tens of thousands of turkeys have drowned and will have to be incinerated. Scores of deer lie dead on the road; a soggy dead deer washes up in the mayor's backyard. We hear an unsubstantiated report of mass escapes from the flooded pens of the illegal alligator farm.

"On the TV they asked this old boy what would be the worst to find when he went back to his house to clean up," Darren tells us, "a gator or a snake? And that ol' boy said he reckoned either one would be pretty bad, but the flat-out worst would be a gator holding a snake."

A state patrol cruiser is totaled when at 70 mph it collides with a vagabond emu.

8

ON THE FOURTH day on the south side of the river, in a parking lot outside the un-flooded mall, a Channel 6 reporter named Lashonda does live-eye standups every hour in front of a tractor-trailer truck filling up with items donated for the flood victims. Smiling volunteers form a bucket brigade, tossing toilet paper, crates of beef-o-roni, cases of processed cheese food while Lashonda, the only black person there, plays cheerleader for the camera. In return for a moment of airtime, the BMW-Mercedes-Audi dealer hands her a check for $1000, and sends Lashonda into the nearby mega-store for a buying spree. We watch her snagging twelve-packs of socks, boxes of crayons and coloring books, an entire display of red and turquoise and gold toothbrushes; she pays with the check, then rolls her buggies outside to be loaded onto the truck. The volunteers circle her, high-fiving and giving thumbs-ups to the camera.

On the fourth day on the north side of the river Claudine and I stand in line all afternoon at the high-school-cum-homeless-shelter with maybe three hundred other people, people who were rescued or evacuated from area trailer parks and migrant camps and rundown rental houses and delivered here on school buses and dump trucks, and we watch a roaring clattering Sikorsky S-80 touch down on the sodden baseball field, in shallow left-center. Before the rotors stop spinning, a squad of National Guard begins to unload and distribute boxes of drinking water. There are three gallon jugs in each box, and each family gets two boxes. Claudine and I give one of ours away. "I need me some Pampers," a woman keeps saying, "I need me some formula and some Pampers." Finally somebody tells her that baby supplies are due in tomorrow. At dusk it starts to drizzle. On the way home we see a huge gray Chinook chuffing low over the treetops, the *whop-whop-whop* of the dual rotors chopping wetly in the rain, the red taillight winking like a jewel.

9

CLAUDINE GIVES UP on calling Lloyd. She spends hours at my computer, writing email, surfing chatrooms, idly flooding the virtual streets of Sim City. I teach her chess; she teaches me backgammon. We play strip poker just for kicks, and after kicks we dress and go next door to see what Darren has to eat. Those whose larders were stocked before the storm are feeding those whose weren't. "All we do is eat and screw and watch TV," Claudine says. "It's about all we *can* do," I say, but we volunteer one day at the high school, passing out Red Cross boxes and helping unload choppers. In the gym, where several hundred families have bunked down on exercise mats and sleeping bags and National Guard cots, they've pulled out one section of bleachers to face a big-screen TV, and that's what most people do all day: watch the flood news on TV, hoping perhaps for a glimpse of their loved ones, their flooded houses, their friends across the river. The Spanish professor with his wretched accent is especially popular among the Latinos as he stumbles over words like "inundated" and "cataclysmic." We watch shots of swirling brown river, the President getting off a helicopter, people's sofas and dining room tables and box-springs floating in their backyards.

The water coming out of our faucets is brown. Claudine and I share a shower anyway. I soap her back, her breasts, under her arms. She rinses off, then suddenly takes hold of me, says, "Excuse me, officer, is this your emu?"

10

THESE TV PEOPLE are crazy for stats. They seek to insulate us from the world by building a wall of numbers. They enunciate precisely, carefully, as if giving out secret equations or passing code. There have been over 200 helicopter rescues per day since noon on Sunday. Across the region some 115,000 people are without power. Some 300 highways, state roads, and secondary roads are closed. The National Guard has deployed over 5,000 troops to control looting. An hour ago the river was at 17.5 feet above flood stage. The river will crest between nine A.M. and noon Tuesday at 28.25 feet. "Who in the fuck is out there measuring the quarter-inches?" Darren wants to know. In Oakboro the mayor has ordered 200 body bags in anticipation of what they'll find when the water goes down. Correction: In Oakboro the mayor has denied that he ordered 200 body bags in anticipation of what they'll find when the water goes down. The Corps of Engineers has used over twelve thousand sandbags in three days. The President's plane will land in another 28 minutes. The 100-year flood plain will need to be revised. This is a 500-year flood. This is a millennium flood. The prime-time male anchor gets into a tiff with one of the reporters who misidentifies a helicopter: It's not a Sikorsky, it's a Huey UH-1. County-wide damage estimates now top $250 million. Statistically speaking, we're beyond disaster and into cataclysm. These are just numbers, the weekend male anchor says, just numbers and they can't begin to tell you anything qualitative about this experience. The bimbo, wearing too much makeup in an attempt to hide her exhaustion, stumbles over numbers. She gets dyslexic; she reads them backwards; she says there's nineteen thousand dollars damage to her Honda when she means nineteen hundred. "Go home and go to bed," Claudine tells the TV.

In the five days and six nights Claudine is here, we make love eleven times.

11

CLAUDINE TELLS ME her nightmare: she was lost in a huge house, she could hear children crying, there was a one-eyed man following her and laughing horribly every time she said something, and then she was naked. "And then you woke me up," she murmurs.

"You were crying," I say, stroking her hair.

She stares at the ceiling. "Just a dream."

We let a moment go by. It's getting light out.

"I still love you, Claudine," I say. "Stupid as it sounds. After all that's happened."

She kisses my shoulder, says she loves me too, but that it doesn't matter. She says we've had our chance and now she needs to try to work things out with Lloyd, if he'll take her back. She says I have to let her go. "You know that, don't you?" she asks me.

The curtains turn milky with morning light. We're holding each other, hardly breathing, it seems to me.

Then Claudine says, "Listen."

I can't hear anything. Birdsong, maybe.

"Hear it?" she says.

"What?"

She rolls over on top of me. "Silence," she says. "No choppers. For the first time in five days, no choppers."

She puts both hands on my shoulders and presses herself down on me, hard. After a minute she says, "That means the bridge is open."

12

TWO MONTHS LATER I see the bimbo bumping a buggy through the Food Lion, working her grocery list with a purple pen. We're navigating in opposite directions, so we meet head-on in every aisle. I almost didn't recognize you, I think of saying—she's in disguise: a sweatshirt, no makeup, and a ponytail—but before I can speak she treats me to a please-don't-say-anything-stupid-to-me smile, so I don't say anything at all. On the next row her co-anchor, in jeans and an untucked flannel shirt, comes around the corner toting a loaf of pumpernickel and a shiny foil bag of salt-&-vinegar chips. He off-loads his loot, looks around, then with one hand pats her fanny fondly. The last I see of them, they're reading ingredients on a jar of garlic-stuffed olives. The bottom rack of their buggy is stacked with sixpacks of Evian.

Wallwork

Sweat

THIS IS WHAT you hear Bernard say as he hangs up the phone: She got me booked two weeks in a row.

It's Regina and the sister in the kitchen with him, and Regina says, Bernard, all right!

She's gonna get me a raise. She says if it all goes good I'll be at six-twenty-five after Thanksgiving. Lookit, she got me booked in Eastland Mall the 26th, 27th, 28th and in Plaza North the 30th and the first. Then maybe next month I'll be going across the river.

You're lying prone on Regina's bedroom floor, pushing putty into baseboard corners. Where the two boards, mitered at a 45-degree angle, don't quite touch.

I knew you could do it, Bernard, Regina says. 'Cause I *know* how you do.

That's right. If I got something I really want, I'll work hard and get it. It's work that gets it. I'm a worker, boy. That's right.

You some hot shit, Bernard, the sister says.

I know it, too.

Bernard.

But see, what I'm worried bout's sweatin. See when I have to talk in front of people I go and break out in sweat. The doctor says it's when I start to talk in front—

You know he been like that all his life.

But she put me on the intercom. See, so I won't have to talk to people, just talk into this mike.

Well how we gonna get to see Bernard? We got to come see you, Bernard. How we gonna get way out there to East Land?

They don't have a car. They take the bus everywhere. The putty's cold and gray in your hand like thick toothpaste. Theirs is the last apartment in the building. You've been putting in new walls for days.

Bernard says it's not bad work. See, I'll carry this brochure 'cause there's just too much to remember. Lookit, see, there's four different models and they all got different features. You know, to keep 'em straight I got to pay attention—

Bernard be talking shit to all these old white women. Hoooeee. Old white women toting shopping sacks. With their diamond *jewels* on. Ah ha ha ha, Bernard.

That's right. Listen. That's right.

Bernard—

Now listen, lemme try it out on you. See. There's lotsa features. You can look down this column, see here, right here, it'll tell you— see this, powerful two-way action, you know, that means it sucks and it sweeps, too.

How much do this cost?

No, see, I don't do that; I'm not a salesman. No. See, I'm a demonstrator. I don't make commission. I get a flat rate per hour. You know. See few wanna buy one, I say, "Very good, that gentleman over there, Mr. Terry Brown, will be happy to take your order for the machine I've just described." See and then Terry Brown takes over and I demonstrate the next one.

Huh.

Yeah, I don't sell. 'Cause see, you a salesman your whole livin depends on what people's buying. Like it snows one day. Nobody's gonna want to buy no vacuum cleaner. And then you don't make no money that day. It's seasonal, sales is seasonal. People don't buy no AC in January. Don't buy ski-jackets in June. But see, I'm on straight salary. So I'll always make *some* money, the same money every day so long as she can book me.

Bernard finally got him a job, the sister says.

Girl, don't you be making fun of Bernard, Regina says. He's gonna be bringing money into this house and that's more than you do.

They've forgotten you're there. You wipe your putty knife backhanded on your overalls and cock your ear.

Shrines

FOR THREE WEEKS you have nailed and sawed, taped and sanded in Regina's third-floor apartment, splattering her verdant wall-to-wall shag with plaster dust and spackle, going goggle-eyed at the new pumpkin paintjob in the living room. Those orange walls! that green floor! and above the TV a strange framed photograph of a horse, with a jumble of vertical and horizontal runes as caption—meaningless when seen straight-on, but take two steps to the side, the lines converge, connect, to spell out the cryptic message JESUS. Christ in code, Jesus on the horsehead.... Before this you worked six days in a house where a woman had lived twenty years tacking every postcard sent her, every pretty magazine picture, every blesséd Catholic newsclipping (*Pope Approves Grape Juice; Primate Blesses Pigs; Our Sister 3, Immaculate Word 2*) through four coats of wallpaper into her ninety-year-old plaster walls. Four red-headed thumbtacks per piece, a thousand holes per wall from waist-high to eye-level, and you fill them all with spackle. Two days it took, and it was so mindless, such desperately dull work, that you charged time-and-a-half and padded your materials double, a pretty penny but still not worth your trouble. Monkeys could have done it. And before that you and Breeze, your assistant, your high school dropout bandana'ed kid assistant, had spent a month re-wiring bathroom light fixtures in a highrise slum apartment building full of Cubans and Haitian refugees. By rights the job was too big for a freelance handyman and his boy go-fer, but you underbid and it helped that you speak *un poco de español*, however poor the grammar.

It is there you first find the shrines. They're all identical: a color Christ on cardboard backing, the kind churches hand out, propped in a corner and ringed by offerings: oil, lit candles, a pan of water, flower petals, a plate of limes. And not a single Cubano who'll look you in the eye. They sing calypso and chant and chatter, and ignore you as you rip from the walls their ancient wiring. You nudge Breeze in the ribs, mutter from the side ot your mouth: See amigo, in voodoo is believed that Jesu, the Christ, he is a powerful spirit, probably the most powerful of all the others. This place is bad news, Breeze says, I can't wait to get outta here.

But you stay in the neighborhood, in this burned-out stretch of city which is too foreboding to support even a pawnshop. On one corner an abandoned grocery (*We Take Food Stamps; Hog Maws $1.09 lb; Hot Head Cheese*). Across the street, Eddie Soul's Marquis Lounge, "Disco Nightly—Up In Here," Closed. Next door is Artie's Liquors, brace of winos attached like suckerfish to sharks. A-1 Donuts—derelict. Laughing Sam's TV Repair—derelict. The derelict House of Beauty, whose sign you often misread from the corner of your eye, because of broken places in the letters, as "House of Reality." There is a chicken wing place and a chop suey joint, the Saigon Inn, and the rest is buck wild and edged as a razorblade, whores and pimps and crackheads and the mailman goes armed; the cops lock their prowl car doors. You're not afraid, as many whites would be, because you never carry money, not even a dollar, and because your face shows not fear or defiance but stoicism; it's a calm, any-age face and it looks in the eye anyone it meets. And because you know the neighborhood.

A Room

HE IS IN a white room, wide white walls. You see him falling again, slow. You were yelling but now you cannot remember what. Scrabble, baby. Scrabble. You slouch on a shiny couch, smoking. Under *Patient's Name*, you printed "B-r-e-e-z-e," then drew a blank.

Regina

REGINA IRONS. SHE watches soaps, *Sanford and Son, The Jeffersons, Family Feud.* Here is how she laughs, a hundred times a day: Ah ha ha ha. Anticipating wrong answers, she yells at game show contestants, You're crazy, white man.

She bakes yams and ribs for supper. She vacuums up your plaster dust daily. She watches *Noon Report* and says the President is too dumb to breathe, even.

She has a little girl, Doowanna, and a stepdaughter. Half-sisters, cousins. A dozen people drop in daily. Her father comes to bum whiskey money. You keep your eyes open, discern blood ties and allegiances. Claudette hates Jackie, Nadine's dad's in jail. But what is Bernard, nephew or lover?

Bernard, Regina says. She stands on tiptoe and kisses his cleft chin. Bernard my boy.

Stories

ONE DAY YOU are sitting at a red light in the truck and two hookers slide up on either side. The windows are down, the heat shimmers off the street, and you look over, grinning, at Breeze. Both women wear onepiece jumpsuits with big gold zippers, and they giggle. Sweet whitemeat! Pull my string. Whatcha got for me today, baby.

You send yours over to the kid's side, two of them leaning in his window, spilling out of their top-heavy suits. Breeze tries to laugh them off and keep their hands away from his crotch. Lemme see what's in your pocket, sugar.

Nothing, Breeze says, smiling hard.

Well I sure feel *some*thing.

Let *me* feel, the other whore says.

You start to laugh. Breeze, you say, you're turning red. Breeze, you're blushing.

Drive, he yells. Just drive on!

One day you're interpreting for Feld, the owner of the voodoo shrine highrise. In the dark lobby you feel Breeze's bad vibes. Feld has collared one of his tenants, and he stands screaming to you: This greasy fucker's been lurking around the building, trying to get a look up some woman's dress, or worse. All day he rides up and down on the elevator and hassles people, all day he's in the halls. I've already had one family move out, living in fear of these Cubans. You speak spick, ask him what the hell he thinks he's up to.

The Cubano looks at you and shows his teeth.

El jefe dice, you say slowly, groping for words. You point to Feld: *El dice, porque es tu en el corridor? Siempre. Si? Todo el dia.*

The Cubano puts his thumb in his nose and turns it.

The women are complaining, Feld says.

Las mujers, no le gustan.

No answer.

Don't you spit on my floor, Jack, Feld says.

The Cubano looks at the wall.

El jefe, no le gusta. Comprende? Shit. I don't think I'm getting through, you say.

Then tell him this, Feld says. Tell him if I catch him harassing anybody again, or loitering out here, or even so much as looking at Mrs. Stovall's little girl again, he'll be out on his ear. He'll be out pronto, his ass'll be out on the street. *Evictado, comprende, Jose?* Tell him that.

But your Spanish has left you.

One day you are eating lunch on the second floor sunporch of an abandoned building and you see a black man detach himself from a group of street people and begin screaming: Stupid niggers! Goddamn apes! You all suck your granny's titties in the sewer water. With both hands he grasps his shirt at the neck and rips it down the front. He flings a broken plastic tricycle against a parked van. He staggers a few feet down the street to tear a young tree in half with a crack like gunshot. Hey, Conan the Barbarian, Breeze says. The people on the stoop are hooting and yelling taunts. One stands and hollers with simple eloquence: Your mama. He is laughing loudly, sarcastically. It's Bernard.

Streets

THESE ARE THE streets you work: Lowery, Spunt, Cooter, Hood. Skinker, which all the natives call Skink. Acme Avenue. Limit Avenue. Pitt Street. Gravois, pronounce the S. The place you live, miles west, is called Earth City. Streets there were named by NASA. Neptune Place. Alan Shepard Circle. Andromeda Court. You explain often that you're not making this up. Apollo Drive, Lunar Drive, Werner Von B Drive. Alpha Centuri Circle. Breeze lives further west, in Carondolet, do not pronounce the T, on a street named by his mother. It was a new development, he explains, and we were already living there when they paved the road and so they asked us to name it. The houses going up around him had lawns the size of football fields, garages big as barns, front porches garnished with pillars, soffits, fluting, fretwork. Breeze's mother wrote down the name for the city cartographers: Plum Nearly Lane.

Ladder

BREEZE IS GOING up with new shingles, he clutches at the gutter, you're bracing with both arms against the rungs, and there's something sharp suddenly at your throat.

This thing's honed fine, a voice says. You know where your carotid artery is?

You nod without looking. Breeze freezes on the ladder.

A different voice says, You ain't got to turn around or nothing.

They lift your wallet and go through it.

All the major credit cards. Two dimes in here for the phone. Stamps, a book of stamps. You loaded for bear, huh whiteman?

Ain't no money?

Hell no. Now what we gonna do with this fool?

Kill him.

What you come down here with no cash for? How you eat?

He got a charge account at Burger King. He scrounge garbage cans. He bring his lunch in a paper poke. Kill him.

Hear that, fool? We kill you for two dimes and a Sears card.

Take my truck, you say. There's a checkbook in the truck. Tools in the back you can hock.

Tools, shit. Truck, shit.

They back up a few steps, then turn to Breeze. Okay, our man on the ladder, one says.

Breeze still looks back over his shoulder. He throws down his wallet. Don't hurt him, you say. He's just a kid.

Shut up.

They kick the ladder out from under him. He's clawing at the roof, legs jerking, shrapnel of nails falling from his tool belt, one torn black shingle flopping down like a broken bird. Scrabble, baby, one of the men cries gleefully.

They knock you down and run.

Doghouse

BRACED BY BRICKS, rust-flecked, ragged-edged oil drum turned on its side. A skinny pup, tied up with swingset chain. A wilderness of glass, shards of brick and concrete, shambles. His muzzle forlornly protruding in the rain.

Spanish

IT IS IMPORTANT to keep saying I did not see him fall. You keep telling yourself this. Look at the walls. But then the doctor is nodding his head and smiling. At Regina's you knocked out a wall with nothing but a 14-ounce hammer and a pry-bar; you built closets, a hall, cleverly added a bedroom, sculpting with sheetrock and two-by-fours, soffits, berms, arches. You lowered a ceiling to cover the new forced-air heating ducts. You laid new tile in the bathroom. Space is fluid, floorplan is, to be reapportioned and subdivided anew, so long as you never knock out load-bearing walls. When the kid had hit the ground you could hear something snap. An ambulance. That is what you were yelling about. Blood was running into your eyes but you could see another man at the end of the alley, a dark Hispanic man listening to you call for help. He had recognized you. He sneered. He called, cuttingly, tough punk voice and spitting slow, as if talking to an idiot, *Las mujers, no le gustan.*

Bernard

MONTHS LATER YOU see him in a huge suburban mall, vast as a stadium, holding a pencil-thin microphone like a conductor's baton and speaking into it the words *stylish* and *variable speed*, slurring the second syllable of *variable*. Sun streams from the skylights two floors above. Women walk from display to display, caressing the sleek machines.

You wait for a break in the monologue and then you shake his hand. Your name is Robinson, you say, and he smiles, puzzled, says that's right, glances down at his nametag: Mr. Robinson. He of course does not remember you. You're wearing a dark suit, you're bare-headed. On impulse you pull his hand, which you still grasp, up to your face, peer at the lines there, knit your brows. Your family calls you Bernard, you say.

That's right, Bernard says. How did you know that?

I see it in your hand. Your mother's name is Regina. Your sister is Claudette. You live uptown, on Ward Street.

Hey, Bernard says, confused.

Your apartment has three bedrooms. The livingroom walls are pumpkin, the shag rug's green. There's a picture of a horse over the TV and a bumpersticker on the bathroom mirror that says JESUS IS YOUR BEST SHOCK ABSORBER. Your mother smokes Winstons, your sister smokes Kools. The landlord's name is Kockle. You have new baseboards in your bedrooms.

Just who the hell are you, Bernard says, jerking his hand away.

When you have to talk in front of people you break out in a sweat. You've been like that all your life.

Bernard's mouth hangs open and you laugh. At first, when you started, you thought you'd explain, when the joke broke down and you could push it no further, that you'd been in the apartment, you'd put in the new baseboards. But now, on impulse, you turn and inexplicably walk away, with Bernard yelling, but only once, Hey, wait!

You don't bother looking back to see if he is following. You go deeper, into the heart of the mall. You know you can lose him, if you need to, in the press of people, in the acres of white floor and wide white walls.

Forgeries

—*A Midsummer Night's Dream*
II, i, 61-82

ALL I TELL you here is lies. Cheap shots, a poetics of vengeance and redress: these are the forgeries of jealousy. You know why I say them.

Jon was poor comfort: "I never know in these situations," I'd say. "Me either, man." "Like are you supposed to let her think you're really broken to pieces? Or that you're perfectly happy without her?" "I know. How are you playing it?"

For a long time now with a burning indifference. It matters nothing to me whom you're sleeping with. But for a year after you left me I lived by hatred. I blurred the first months with pills, J&B, and minute quantities of uncut cocaine—the classic phase of self-destruction. I can hear you laughing: so predictable, the clichés, the histrionics. It was a sham, of course. And I knew it. A little effort took me outside, let me step off and watch myself—with a contemptful bemusement—playing out the B-movie of my life without you. A study in irony and self-hatred. I modified one of your favorite catchphrases: Although hate is not good for the soul, the body at least shows no ill effects. And built one of my own: To love is to lose self-reliance.

I keep, even now, so long since we have even spoken, a perverse kind of shrine. Photos on the wall. A bottle of massage oil I will never again open. Your lemon candle on the headboard: a soft seductive glow. The blue terrycloth robe—the first gift you ever bought me—drapes over a chair by my nightstand; the women who eventually learn each detail of our tangled past, the chronology of your treachery, slip gently in and out of that robe on nightly treks from bed to bathroom and back.

The women: O yes: since the time of our last lovemaking I have slept with nineteen different women, each bedding marked by a gentleness and passion you never showed me in all our five years of adolescent humping. Every one of them was, in her own way, a better lover than you were; all but one lauded me: a good man is hard to find. O yes. (The one abstention from this consensus shared your surname, by the way—unfortunate coincidence, but I didn't find out until later—and she seemed to feel nothing from the neck down anyway.) Of my many lovers you hold two distinctions: you were the first, and you were the dullest.

(Remember, these are forgeries.)

A week after you left me the third and final time for your busboy high school dropout, at a party where they poured Quaaludes into candy dishes like mints and couples balled on the back porch chaise lounges, I intruded on a kindred soul. Exploring upstairs, I found Jon in the master bedroom consoling a Panamanian cellist. The cellist had been snorting coke and crying. "My friend Miguel," Jon explained. "Having problems with his girlfriend." "My heart," Miguel said, not looking up, "man, she hurt my heart. She treat me like a shit, like a turt." I could not read Jon's expression. "The guy she is with, he cannot satisfy her. She come back to me, sleep with me and tell me this. But where is she tonight, bitch?" Closing the door behind me I heard him say, "She *tell* me he cannot get an erection."

Ah, Miguel. I laugh now, notwithstanding the irony, but for a while there I played it, as Jon would say, with a truly fucked mania. Following you both around town. Calling and hanging up. Waiting for a chance to say to your face that I'd never take you back. Forswearing your bed and company. I xeroxed the best of your letters, blacking out my name, and left copies everywhere.

The bank. Museums. Restaurants. Some I mailed out to friends. I shaved off the beard you loved so well. To spite my own face. I took photos. At Belk you swirled around the cosmetics case, gasping, "What are you doing here?" And, "A Nikon—when did you get that?" Noncommittal, I fired, advanced, fired, advanced, caught you baking up, focused and fired again. And then left. Those photos: small eyes wide, a tight smile, your pores huge and grainy because in my hate—in my *haste*—I had misread the light meter. An indicator.

Too shaken for another encounter of that sort, I tracked you both by telephoto the rest of the week. From parked cars I shot him slouching out of the restaurant in his stained apron; from the yard next door I framed you greeting him one night on your front steps—ill met by porchlight. Rash, wanton, tugging by his beltloop, you led him inside, cut the lights and laid him on the couch of your mother's dark living room. It took a long time. Prepared, I had loaded Jon's Nikon with infrared film and covered the flash unit with a red filter—the flare was invisible. The photos showed later that your eyes were closed anyway. I can't say why I felt it so much: it took a long time.

Every word of this is forgery. Each syllable catches false in my throat. These are the lies, the faiths which sustain me through this miserable life without you. I have the negatives and several sets of prints. You know where to reach me.

Balm

ON THEIR THIRD day as lovers, eleven days after her second miscarriage, they moved out of the guest room into the master bedroom—the room decorated with snapshots of her husband in camies leaning against a Humvee, beach photos from their Antigua honeymoon, studio portraits of her in-laws, the room whose sliding glass door opened to a south-facing balcony that got the daylong sunlight—and she led him by the hand and together they turned down the bed without speaking and she lay back and saw him hesitate only a moment, so she sat up and took his face in both hands and pulled him down on top of her. They were naked from the shower and damp and they kissed for several minutes. When he sat up she handed him a yellow jar labeled BALM. The white blinds were open and the sun, he remembered from a Joni Mitchell song, poured in like butterscotch, and he unscrewed the jar and dipped out a dollop of thick sticky honey-colored stuff and lifted her bare foot to his mouth and kissed it, then began massaging the balm into the balls of her feet and between her unpainted toes. He did both feet and both ankles and both calves and her thighs and he took his time, thinking with his eyes closed the word *bliss*. The room smelled of honey and sex and he stopped to read the ingredients on the jar: *Organic Honey, Shea Butter. All Natural. Apply Liberally.*

She was breathing deeply, almost swooning. He looked at her breasts, her closed eyes, her mouth, her breasts, her tan belly.

A round mirror hung above the headboard. He could see his

worn unshaven face in the bright morning but he couldn't see her at all and he thought it an odd place for a mirror.

He applied balm to the sides of her thighs, to her hipbones, to her belly.

I don't like this bed, he said after a while.

She kept her eyes closed. This is my bed, baby, she murmured. I picked it out. I've had this bed since before I even met him.

Gratefully, he bent to kiss between her parted legs.

Not yet, she said. Balm me. Balm the rest of me.

Though her eyes were closed she could tell he was smiling. What? she said.

Can you use "balm" as a verb?

Of course. In this bed balm is a verb.

Because she loved words and loved to be touched she had let the saleswoman in BodyWorks massage the balm into her open palm, listening to her quote from the label: "balm: (1) an aromatic preparation (as a healing lotion); (2) a soothing restorative agency"; she said it was an ancient word, they had balm back in the Bible, honey, did you know that? It fixes what ails you. An eight-ounce jar was $20.

The room smelled thickly of honey and lightly of sex and when she couldn't lie still any longer she took the jar from him and turned him face down and began balming his back, long slow strokes as she bent low, brushing her breasts and hair against him and feeling his buttocks clinch under her hips. In the bright sun she saw a line of three evenly spaced freckles across his left shoulderblade and she saw a brown birthmark the shape of a blackberry under his arm; she was still learning his body, as he was hers. She knew he had noticed her imperfections: her right breast larger than her left, her botched appendectomy scar, her crooked front tooth, and she loved him already for dividing his attention evenly between both breasts and resting his cheek against the scar the first time he told her he loved her and for licking her teeth when they kissed, and she

knew in the honey-smelling light that she loved him too although
she had yet to say it aloud, and she also knew she was going to be
in a very very bad place when he went back to his wife and when
her husband was rotated home, but—now? he said, now? and then
Now, and he turned her back over and put his mouth over hers—
for now it was all light and honey and balm, necessary and healing
and without which there would be emptiness, nothingness, which
had somehow been bearable until now, but after this she wouldn't
know anything; she didn't know what she would or could do, but
now it was all balm, yellow all over the blue sheets and their legs
and arms and everywhere else, and she closed her eyes again and
whispered to him, Yes.

Boy Poets

WE WERE BOY poets, Bouchard and I, fools, wild for words, idiots, aloof and condescending. Between algebra and art we stalked the dim halls of our decrepit high school, scuffing our feet and screaming to no one but ourselves "Radio belly! Cat shovel!" or "Don't let that horse! Eat that violin!" or "Ink runs from the corners of my mouth! There is no happiness like mine! I have been eating poetry!" We tried to check out every volume of poems in our molding library, two-and-a-half shelves full, and when the poor librarian disallowed it—there was a six-book takeout limit—we got all our friends to check them out for us; we annihilated those shelves, razed them like some nuclear ground zero, left only a forlorn Rod McKuen fallen flat in the dust. We had friends but no peers, none. Out of fifteen-hundred-and-seventy-six students, eighteen English teachers, and a bald-headed seven-foot-tall principal with a Ph.D., we were the only ones who knew a trochee from an anapest, the only ones who correctly pronounced the tricky names of Yeats, Keats, and Roethke, the only ones who knew Joyce Kilmer was a guy and Elizabeth Bishop was a lesbian. Bouchard would say Man, you know that color of city bus windows lit from inside at night, how come you can't get that color into a poem, and I'd say Man, it's the same color as the light coming up through the deep end of a swimming pool at midnight if you were seeing it from an airplane at 20,000 feet, you could write it like that, and he'd say Let's go to the mother-fuckin hockey game and watch those morons beat the snot out of each other and write poems about it on the backs of popcorn boxes, and by God that's what we did. Or we'd sneak out to the Waffle House at 2:30 A.M. and sit over rubbery scrambled eggs and ketchup and stare past each other like zombies and scrawl on napkins lines of poems about scrambled eggs and zombies wearing rubbers and use up one napkin and throw it aside and start another one and so on until our booth looked like the littered desk in *Doctor Zhivago*, the scene where Omar Sharif tears through page after page of *The Laura Poems*, writing and rewriting and rewriting again a whole book in a single snowbound night, Julie Christie naked and well-fucked and zonked under furs in the next room, and the good doctor on fire with poetry, like we were, a blizzard of napkins torn and twisted with the ravings of our boy poet muses until the waitress would throw us out, screaming "Next time you come in here bring a G.D. notebook, you idiots," and Bouchard bowing and blowing her a kiss and saying that as best he could tell, her ass under the baggy brown Waffle House slacks must surely sing like a sonnet, or better yet a villanelle, or maybe her bottom was just a metaphor for pure divine perfection—ass-crazy Bouchard. He had a beige 1961 Plymouth station wagon that for a while we called The Ply-Mouth, as in a mouth made of plywood, and then he got a job clerking at a bookstore and filled the backseat of The Ply-Mouth with stolen volumes of poetry and tracts on Zen and Bob Dylan sheetmusic and Vonnegut novels and coffee-table books of Japanese erotic art, and so then we started calling it The Billy Bouchard Book-Mobile, and he would drive with me steering while he shifted gears and leafed through the latest issue of *Poetry* or *APR* or *The New Yorker* and he would find a poem and start screaming it out the rolled-down window while I did my best to keep us from running up on the sidewalk and flattening somebody's grandpa, Jesus Christ, Bouchard.

In our Russian history class we learned about the 1670 failed revolt led by a serf named Stenka Razin, how on the way to his execution he was paraded through the streets of St. Petersburg in an oxcart and the populace poured over his head what our textbook politely called "buckets of filth," so for our senior project in Russian

History, Bouchard and I composed a thirty-seven page chapbook of poems about Lenin at the Finland Station and Ivan the Terrible and Puskin and Catherine the Great moaning under that horse and Karl Marx and Anna Akhmatova and Yevtushenko and the famous serf revolutionary martyr Stenka Razin and we titled our book *A Bucket of Filth*, and it came back with a grade I swear to God of 92-and-one-half points, a half point shy of being an "A," and the teacher's upright cursive red-ink comment: "Interesting."

We studied with a visiting poet named Peters who on the first day showed a short film about James Dickey called *Barnstorming for Poetry* in which Dickey swore poetry was "the greatest goddamn thing in the universe," went deer hunting with a bow and arrow, played 12-string guitar with students at a party, got drunk and read his poems to an auditorium of college freshmen who would rather be watching *Gilligan's Island* reruns, and that was it. That was it for us. We were in, all the way. Peters had some kind of neurological disorder that made his left eye twitch every four or five seconds; it must have driven him mad but surely it made him a better poet by infusing everything he did and said with richness and ambiguity, which we first understood when he read us a lament that began "Nothing can top the irony of losing your heart to a lesbian" and the whole time he was winking, he looked up after reading that line and winked with a frown on his face, and Bouchard and I started winking back, and we deliberately winked from then on through every poem we ever read aloud until we stopped noticing that we were doing it and then realized we were and then couldn't stop. We went to open mic poetry readings and tried out our winking verses on unsuspecting underage hippie girls and dancers and high-school actresses, and half the time they'd wink back out of confusion or some kind of empathetic disorder, and after that it was easy to seduce them. I wrote a two-page poem about how after a poetry reading I took a sixteen-year-old girl out to the parking lot where in the backseat of my dad's pumpkin-colored Pontiac she slapped my face for giving her a hickey on her bare belly, and Bouchard wrote a five-page poem about how I wrote a two-page poem about a sixteen-year-old girl slapping my face for giving her a hickey on her bare belly.

There was a girl, Colleen Gilfillian, a beautiful Black Irish girl with dark hair to her waist and dark gypsy eyes who was that most unlikely thing: an honor roll cheerleader; she was vice-president of the senior class and president of the Thespians and suffered "President Lesbian" jokes with grace and wit, and due to her perfect diction and ability to sight-read scripts was the student who did the daily PA announcements during homeroom; Bouchard and I used to go to the football games and hide under the bleachers and howl out lines of our poems, including "Football Is A Fascist Conspiracy" and a haiku sequence that began "inflated brown skin / of slaughtered innocent pig / vomits through night air"—don't bother counting the syllables, we knew what the fuck we were doing—and one night Colleen dragged us out from under there saying we were trying to sneak looks up the cheerleaders' micro-miniskirts and we said Jesus Christ, can't you see we're under here barnstorming for poetry? and besides, the way y'all jump around like a bunch of drunken kangaroos, who has to *sneak* looks? The kangaroo simile was Bouchard's, by the way. Our point was that the color-coordinated underpants were clearly part of the uniform and were *deliberately designed to be seen* with every leg kick and bent-over butt-wiggle, so we had her there, and she, a lover of logic rumored to have scored the second-highest SAT that year, instantly saw our point and apologized. This was a girl who had won a Morehead scholarship to Duke and had turned down dates with the first-string quarterback, the second-string quarterback, the tight end, two wide receivers, and three running backs but had gone on a mercy date with a dumb but sweet second-string right guard and left his head spinning, and Bouchard and I took her off in the Bookmobile that night and kept her out past her curfew and seduced her with the corrupting influence of Japanese erotic art and poetry. We absolutely destroyed her life, took her after midnight to the CSX switching station and crawled up into empty boxcars and spread out a blanket and drank MD 20/20 straight from the bottle and read poems to her in the moonlight while all around us trains crashed and coupled and decoupled and made their metallic shrieks, and the very night itself and all its sounds were poetry. My poems took liberty with structure, featured slant rhymes like "silver" and "lover," used lower-case letters like e.e. cummings, indented lines randomly or centered them by painstakingly counting letters and spaces on an IBM Selectric and dividing by two; years before rap was invented I wrote a rap poem that looked on the page like an exploded James Brown lyric but on closer examination scanned perfectly as eighteen lines of dactylic hexameter; but Bouchard was wilder than that: he threw out the rule book *a la* Whitman, he never counted a syllable or rhymed if he could help it, he'd break a line anywhere, even on an "and" or a "but" or even in the middle of a word, and that's what Colleen fell for. She was our Julie Christie. He had her five months, and a week before graduation I took her away from him and he never spoke to me again or as far as I know wrote another line of poetry, and two years later he was late to work and stepped in front of a city bus in downtown Atlanta and I didn't hear about it for a month after.

And then it was an impossible twenty-five years later, like forever and like overnight, and there they were, the bald ancient principal, the now-bald senior class president, the still-a-dork guidance counselor, and Colleen, divorced, childless, in a baggy black cardigan and khakis and flat shoes—all of them onstage at our high school reunion taking turns with a blue screwdriver undoing the lid of a homemade time capsule and pulling out thing after thing: a pristine yellow yearbook, a pair of brand new 25-year-old bluejeans, a hall pass, a Cat Stevens album. And then Colleen said that she'd like to remind us all that our class had been blessed to have had not one but two poet laureates, both of whom had collaborated on the time capsule poem, that she herself had been present when they'd written it, had watched them alternating lines, composing what she knew we would all agree was a profound and beautiful expression of our youth in its first blossom, and then she was calling my name, calling me up onstage, handing me a single sheet of parchment covered with my quarter-century-old back-slanted scrawl and Bouchard's block letter capitals, and there I was holding a poem I had forgotten existed, let alone had any memory of writing. The bald class president raised up the microphone and Colleen stood one step behind me with her sad hand on my shoulder and I read the first four-and-a-half lines and my eyes filled up and I was blind, blind like Robert Frost snow-blinded at JFK's inauguration, unable to see, the words sliding off into the margins; I couldn't read it, and then when I could, I wouldn't, and I sat down and folded the poem in half and then folded it again and put it in the breast pocket of my blue suit and left the reunion early. It's mine: the only extant copy of the Eastbrook High Class of '75 time capsule poem. I have it with me now, right here, but I'm not going to try to read it again, ever. Not even to you.

The Secret University

1975

1

Ah, poetry: what secret doors might it unlock? In the hip pocket of Loflin's stiff new blue jeans is a single sheet of buff-colored bond, a typed poem precisely folded into fourths. The poem begins "When I sleep / I dream that I am sleeping / and dreaming I am asleep...", lines that precocious Loflin, boy poet, had composed in high school four, no, five years ago, and then had set aside until now, this very afternoon, a lifetime later, when he had managed to squeeze out another eight lines before scrawling at the bottom a flourished *fin*. Loflin had a special spot for his compositions *al fresco*: under a big loblolly pine in the woods by the campus archery range. The old tree shielded him from the occasional wayward arrow skittering through the weeds, and except when the marching band used the adjacent field for practice, pumping out their tuba-heavy versions of "Purple Haze" and "Sunshine of Your Love," Loflin liked to write there; it was not far from his dorm, so he could rush back up the hill and type up whatever lines he managed to eek out, and the arrows *seemed* more dangerous than they were and somehow inspired him. Today he had been working under pressure, for Elizabeth had told him only two things: he must be on time, and he must bring a new poem.

So here he was. Up an outdoor flight of steel fire-escape stairs, through a jimmied metal door with its bolt duct-taped over, down a brief hall of unprimed drywall: Loflin followed Elizabeth's directions and found himself standing before a dark door the color of walnut, peering into a small pane of stained glass glowing vermillion and verdigris. Poet colors, he thought. The door was cracked open and a white index card push-pinned above the knob bore the tiny typed word *poetry*, a bit off-center. He patted his hip pocket and pushed the door wide, smiling.

On his mental map of campus Loflin located this door in Hall B of the west wing of the second floor of the Publications Building, a building that he knew had started life as the chancellor's horse stable, and then, after horses were banned from campus in 1934, had been converted in turn to a cafeteria, a mail-sorting-facility-combination-laundry, a temporary dorm for overflow GI Bill students, the first campus police station, and finally a storage facility that also housed university publications, including the student poetry magazine. A magazine that had so far rejected every poem Loflin had ever submitted.

2

INSIDE THE OFFICE a young woman sitting in a blue papasan chair looked up from her book, frowning: "You're late." "Do I know you?" Loflin said. He realized almost as soon as he had said it that he was speaking to his former freshman composition teacher, a graduate student named Cherry whom he had not seen since the final exam two years ago. He apologized immediately, explaining that he was somewhat nearsighted and hadn't recognized her dressed like that. In class Cherry had worn jeans and sweaters and the occasional pantsuit, hardly memorable, but here it seemed she had gone in for the femme fatale look in a big way: black boots and a black leather miniskirt, and she had dyed her hair, too, he saw: a kind of chestnut red with cherry-colored (of course, he thought) highlights. When one is only twenty years old, someone twenty-five or twenty-six can seem infinitely more worldly, and perhaps this accounted for some of Loflin's feelings of unease, but there was something else stirring in him as well, something awkward and worried. Something in him thought he should say right away, "I have a girlfriend, you know," perhaps "Apropos of nothing, I have a girlfriend," or even "My girlfriend would like those boots." Instead he asked, "Where's Elizabeth? I thought she'd be here." "She's upstairs," Cherry said. "Did you bring your poem? Let me see it." Loflin fished it out of his hip pocket and held it up, raising his eyebrows. "Good," Cherry said, "let's scoot. We don't want to keep the others waiting." "What others?" Loflin said. "Come on," Cherry said, and she stood and waved him over to a narrow steel ladder half-hidden by a corner bookcase, a ladder that started three feet from the floor and went up to what he could now see was a trapdoor in the ceiling. "It's a bit of a reach for the first rung," Cherry explained, "so just stand on this," and with a slight effort she slid a *Webster's Unabridged Dictionary of the English Language* into place with her boot-toe. "You've got to be kidding," Loflin said, looking at the ladder; he had a deathly fear of heights. "Go on," she said. "You first," Loflin told her. She blinked at him. "Hey, this ain't no porn show," she said. "Go up a ladder in a miniskirt with a guy behind me? I don't *think* so. Nice try, buster." "No, no, no, that's not—" Loflin said, but Cherry just pointed up, smirking.

He returned the folded poem to his hip pocket and mounted the dictionary.

3

AT THE TOP of the ladder he found Elizabeth was waiting for him; she gave him her hand and pulled him onto a narrow catwalk suspended on steel cables. He looked down into darkness, but had a sense of a vast open space below him, and he shuddered. Glancing back down the ladder he saw Cherry emerging from the trapdoor and realized he was staring directly down her blouse; so much for the porn show, he thought. He extended his hand but Cherry took Elizabeth's instead. The two women replaced the foam ceiling panel that had concealed the trapdoor. "Onward," Elizabeth whispered, switching on a dim penlight. She led the way across the catwalk.

As a boy, Loflin had suffered the sheerest terror of his life on the swinging bridge at Grandfather Mountain, and although this was not as bad—for he still couldn't see what sort of abyss they dangled over—he definitely felt the catwalk swaying. He put his hand lightly on Elizabeth's shoulder, for reassurance, and his other hand he reached back toward Cherry, in case she wanted to take it, but of course she didn't.

At the other end of the catwalk they came to a heavy steel door featuring the first keypad combination lock Loflin had ever seen. Elizabeth punched a few numbers and hit "enter" and the door buzzed open. "How did y'all find out the code?" Loflin asked. "What do you mean? It's our code," Elizabeth told him, but Cherry shushed her and ushered them inside.

They were in a large well-lit room. In front of Loflin stood two new young women, one black and one white, and behind them was a wall of floor-to-ceiling shelves that bore a hundred brown and yellow human skulls.

4

"This is Alyssa," Elizabeth said, pointing to the black girl, "and this is Latisha." The white girl smiled at him. "This is David Loflin, y'all." Latisha and Alyssa did a synchronized curtsey and Loflin thought it one of the weirdest things he'd ever seen. He noticed that Alyssa was wearing a denim skirt and a khaki blouse, and Latisha was wearing a denim blouse and a khaki skirt, but before he could remark on this, Latisha pulled a grinning skull from a shelf, and Alyssa leaned toward Loflin and made quote marks in the air with her curled fingers, and Latisha intoned, "Alas, poor Yorick! I knew him, Horatio, a fellow of infinite jest—" "Come on, you guys," Elizabeth interrupted; "We're late. We have to hurry."

"What *is* this place," Loflin asked, as Cherry gave him a little shove toward the door. "It's a secret archeology lab," she said. "These are Indian skulls, from the Chowan burial ground they've been excavating since the '60s." "Why is it secr—" "Because the Indian activists consider these skulls stolen property. If this location wasn't secret, they'd break in here and steal them back. Do you know what I mean?" "I think so," Loflin said. He wanted to linger, looking at her there in her black boots and miniskirt—Cherry his docent, his dreamgirl guide to the secret university—but already Elizabeth was leading Alyssa and Latisha down a flight of stairs and out of sight; he and Cherry had to scramble to catch up.

At the bottom of the stairs they entered a dingy passageway, flaking gray-green walls lit by bare overhead bulbs. Steam pipes dangled from the ceiling, hissing softly. "Watch your head," Elizabeth called back. They hurried down the corridor and hung a right. "This is the experimental animal nursery," Cherry said as they came to a door labeled RESTRICTED AREA BIOL FAC & GRAD STDNTS ONLY. Through a plate glass window beside the door Loflin was able to see several rows of cages of white mice and a single pen holding a forlorn Chihuahua. "Jesus Christ," he said. "They *raise* them here? People feed them and take care of them and then—" and Cherry said, "Do you have any idea how many white mice this university cuts up every single day? It doesn't make sense to buy them when you can breed them." "Come on, you two," Elizabeth said, taking another turn.

In the next room, they interrupted a figure drawing class that appeared to have no professor. The model, a young woman Loflin recognized as last year's runner-up for Homecoming Queen, stared at them a moment, then stood and crossed her arms over her breasts and turned her back. "Sorry," Elizabeth called as they backed out; "wrong turn."

In the next hallway they detoured around a pile of broken mannequins, plastic arms and legs all intertwined.

They passed an open archway and Loflin stopped to peer in. He saw several dozen upright pianos, tan and black and brown, and two baby grands, all crammed together tightly as tenement houses. He took a step in, pressed a key: E above middle C. No sound. He glanced at Cherry. "The piano graveyard," she said, and shrugged. "You know the university owns hundreds of pianos. And employs a full-time piano tuner. Well, these are pianos that couldn't be tuned. So they go off to the graveyard to die." Loflin flashed on images of elephants and ivory. "They store extra sonatas in here too," Cherry said mysteriously, "but they're all boxed away and you can't see them."

"Somewhere around here is a room filled waist-high with deflated basketballs," Latisha said, and Alyssa made the quote marks in the air around her sentence.

"And a human-scale maze for psych experiments," Elizabeth said. "And also there's a room full of boxes of saltines from the 1950s."

"Where are we going?" Loflin asked.

"To the poetry room, of course," Cherry said.

"And where are we right now?" Loflin asked. "I mean, what building are we under?"

No one answered.

5

IT IS AN occupational hazard for writers that life imitates art, and now, as Loflin realized he was lost (the steam passage ran perpendicular to the catwalk, he figured, but after the Animal Nursery he'd become disoriented and the corridor had curved, so he had no idea which of a dozen campus buildings they were now under, or in fact, whether they were even under a building or just in some kind of secret tunnel system), he began to feel like a character in some fairy tale, and he wished he'd left a trail of bread crumbs on the forest floor, or unrolled his string more carefully as he wandered the labyrinth. He thought of Borges, and of Poe—of Poe's motifs of concealment and burial, of Borges's infinite labyrinths and libraries—and just as he thought the word "libraries," Cherry turned and smiled and pointed through a doorway, and said softly, "Look."

They were passing a room of books, thousands and thousands of books stacked floor to ceiling with tiny aisles left between them. "This is where they keep the overdue books," Cherry told him. "What do you mean?" Loflin said; "overdue books are overdue because they're checked out; they wouldn't be here." "These are the *actual* books," Cherry said. "The ones in the library are just facsimiles, and when the facsimiles become overdue, the actual ones are transferred here. Do you see what I mean?" "Maybe," Loflin said; "I'm not sure. Kind of like a lost and found?" "Not really, but I guess that's close enough," Cherry said. "What did you make in my class? B-minus?" "B-plus," Loflin said. "Huh," Cherry said.

What in hell had he been thinking, when Elizabeth had first invited him? Show up at midnight, bring a poem? He thought of his girlfriend, at another university on the other side of the state, and wondered how she'd feel about him wandering the bowels of the earth at midnight with four strange women. He had no idea what was happening here.

"I bet you don't know what this is," Cherry said, gesturing grandly into the darkness.

"You're right," Loflin told her.

"It's cyberspace."

"Cyberspace."

"Exactly. This is the real thing. It hasn't even been invented yet, really—it won't be invented until, oh, about 1985—but here it is. Cyberspace. Just waiting to be invented. Do you know what I mean?"

"No," Loflin said. "I don't know. I don't know what you mean at all."

"Just remember you saw it here first," Cherry said.

6

PAST CYBERSPACE THEY came to a corner alcove, a kind of passageway nook furnished with leather armchairs and a few fringed floor pillows. "Poetry room," Elizabeth announced as she slipped into a chair. Loflin watched Cherry in her miniskirt sink gracefully onto a blue pillow, legs folded to the side; he tried not to ogle but was not entirely successful. "Let's have a poem," she said, staring him down, and Elizabeth pulled from her jacket pocket a small hardbound notebook, vermillion and verdigris, and opened it and said, "Okay, but it's kind of surrealistic," and then began to read, in a soft but steady voice:

> *When I sleep*
> *I dream that I am sleeping*
> *and dreaming I am asleep...*

Loflin, dumbfounded, felt his mouth literally drop open and waited for something to come out, but nothing did. He reached into his hip pocket and felt the folded edge of the only copy in the world of the poem he had written that afternoon. "That poem," he started to say, "that poem—" "Is awful," Cherry said. "Really, Elizabeth, what a trite idea, what a maudlin attempt at surrealism, where's your deep image, where's the teacup covered with fur, for God's sake?" and while Elizabeth smiled at him, Loflin decided this whole thing was a dream, start to finish, just a weird, wacked-out semi-nightmare, and he was ready to wake up now—Wake up now, he told himself, it was fun while it lasted, but let's wake up now—a dream-technique that heretofore had always worked, but this time, nothing happened, or actually, something did happen, but not what Loflin was hoping for. Fifty yards down the corridor a door opened and a campus cop stuck his head through and caught sight of them and yelled, like a dumb cop in a dumb TV sitcom, *"Hey, you kids!"*

In slow motion Cherry turned her face toward Loflin; he watched the corners of her mouth twitch up in a smile: Isn't this fun? she seemed to be saying. Then she was on her feet and reaching for his hand, and Elizabeth was screaming *"Run!"* and then they were running, all of them, and sliding around the corner and splitting up at Cherry's direction: Elizabeth ducked into an alcove full of folding chairs; Latisha and Alyssa ran down a side passage toward an opening labeled LAUNDRY CHUTE. "Come on," Cherry cried, and pulled him farther down the hall. Loflin heard the cop, some distance away, yelling his ridiculous "Stop or I'll shoot!" They kept running. They ran down a half-flight of stairs two at a time. They passed through an enormous storage room. Things began to blur. They ran past bound copies of the Chancellor's Mission Statement. In peripheral vision Loflin glimpsed random images: enormous spools of fiber-optic cable, jars of fetal pig hearts. He saw a sled emblazoned with the word ROSEBUD and he heard a steel door crash shut behind them. They ran past a wind tunnel. Cherry's boots pounded madly against the concrete floor. They went flying by a dozen riding lawnmowers and rows of stainless steel canisters of neodymium. Loflin heard the cop shouting into his walkie-talkie. "Hurry!" Cherry screamed. They ran past a Greek Chorus, a bundle of blunt arrows, a scale model of the Parthenon. They passed Op Art and the Empty Set. They passed Willie M. and parameciums in agar-agar and they passed the music of the spheres.

Loflin heard gunshots and a scream. They kept running. They ran deeper and deeper. They ran past a metaphor and a simile having tea in fur-lined teacups. They ran past the dustbin of history and the id, the ego, and the superego. They passed Special Relativity and supply-side economics and they passed the patriarchy and an igneous outcrop and double-entry accounting. They ran past Ockham's Razor. They passed the place where they kept the Pythagorean Theorem. "Hurry, hurry!" Cherry whispered. A door slammed closed behind them. They came to a dead end, a damp and crumbling brick wall. They were trapped, he thought, trapped like rats, like white lab rats. And then all his clichés left him.

"Now," Cherry said, "now," she whispered, pressing him against the wall; he could smell her cherry hair and her lips on his ear, and he saw behind her the cop come huffing and chugging around the corner— "*now,* tell me your poem."

And that was when it happened. For the first time in his life, Loflin became a poet. He opened his mouth. He found his voice. He spoke.

Marianne Moore's Tricorn Hat

ON THE DAY he turns fifty, he is teaching for the first time a selection of poems by Marianne Moore to a class of slack-ass graduate students, people sliding through an M.A. on their way to working the latte machine at Borders or teaching part-time at a community college, people who hate each other because they've had too many writing workshops where they tore each other to shreds and taught themselves a finely-tuned contempt for any written word not their own. The professor arrives late because he'd forgotten and had to return to his office for his visual aid—a dramatic black-and-white portrait, downloaded from the Academy of American Poets website, of Marianne Moore in black cape and tricorn hat. He likes to begin each class with a bit of memorable trivia, just to get the discussion going, so as he plops into his swivel chair at the head of the seminar table, he slides the photo to the student who sits to his left, actually his favorite student in the class, the only non-English major, a newly divorced mother of two who's back in school studying biology but who loves poetry enough to take an overload this semester, and she picks up the portrait and gives it a long look with one eyebrow raised. The professor opens his manila folder, shuffles through a few pages, then finds what he wants. He clears his throat, glances at his divorced biologist, looks over to the hippie kid with his ponytail and little John Lennon spectacles, pans the rest of the room: the ex-Marine ex-firefighter whose new expertise is war poetry; the twins, Terri and Sherri; Wanda, the wistful young woman obsessed with Sylvia Plath—some of them nod at him and he nods back, then says, "Okay, here's today's pointless literary fun fact," and then looks down at the page in front of him and reads this: "In the twentieth century, perhaps no article of poet's clothing in the English-speaking world was as famous as Marianne Moore's hat, in which she was photographed for *Life, The New Yorker,* and *The New York Times,* and which she wore at many public functions where she acted as hostess to the mayor of New York City. As her fame grew, her black cape and tricorn hat became her trademark. In one interview she claimed to like the shape of her hats because—and I'm quoting here, people—'they conceal the defects of my head, which resembles that of a hop toad'."

He looks up and sees that the photo has reached his ponytailed student, who takes it by one corner, squints at it, and passes it on, muttering, "Man, that is so *gay.*"

The professor, who is himself gay but not out, certainly not with his students anyway, begins to explain that unlike some poets they've studied, Miss Moore's work does not reference sexual orientation or identity politics, and so the question of which way she went is not germane, but the ex-Marine interrupts and says "Well, she never got married, did she? I mean, why do they always refer to her as *Miss* Moore? And didn't H.D. publish Moore's first book, and wasn't Moore friends with Elizabeth Bishop? Because we know that both of *them* were lesbians," and the biology major says "Well, she was friends with Wallace Stevens too, and I'm pretty fucking sure that *he* wasn't a lesbian, you ass," and the professor cuts them off, saying, "People, please, christ, it's only February, at this rate we'll never make it through the semester without killing each other. Please please please raise your hand when you have a comment and let me call on you." The ponytailed student raises his hand. "I have a comment," he says. "Go ahead," the professor says. "I think you misunderstood my previous comment," he says; "I didn't mean that Marianne *Moore* was gay, I meant that her *hat* was gay, like totally gay, like, in the sense of lame or uh pathetic, you know, like geeky. Like that."

The biology student raises her hand and the professor, grateful, hopeful, calls on her. She turns to Ponytail and says, "In the sense of lame or uh pathetic, you know, like geeky, I think *you're* gay."

By this time the portrait has come all the way around the room to the student on the professor's right, a young man who will not only never finish his thesis but never even decide on a thesis topic, and this student says, "She looks like George Washington crossing the Mississippi."

After that, they read Marianne Moore's poem "An Egyptian Pulled Glass Bottle in the Shape of A Fish."

BECAUSE THE PROFESSOR is between boyfriends, he eats his birthday dinner with his lovely silver-haired mother. She has fried up a mess of squash, cut so thin and battered in a bit of flour and pepper and hot and crisp like something you might eat in heaven, and cornbread and molasses and slaw and blackeyed peas, and iced tea, the elixir of the gods. He tells his mother about Marianne Moore's hat, and his mother says she remembers the pictures in *Life* magazine. "She wore a cape, too, didn't she?" his mother asks. The professor nods and says that in fact, Miss Moore's very first cape was made for her by her own mother, for when she went off to college; her mother wanted her to cut a dashing figure on the Bryn Mawr campus. "Remember those shirts I sewed you for college?" his mother asks. The professor does remember them, hideous western-style shirts with snaps instead of buttons, denim and undyed canvas fronts and backs with contrasting cuffs and yokes made of patterned prints—paisleys, cornflowers. They talk about the shirts, laughing. They talk about a yellow cashmere sweater his mother had in high school. They do not talk about whether Marianne Moore was a lesbian. They wash up the dishes together, the professor drying, and then he makes his wish and blows, hard, hard, 50 candles is almost too many but with a last gasp he gets them, and they eat wax-pocked cake in the den with *Soul Hits of the 60s* on the portable CD player. "I remember when you were just a baby," his mother says, which sounds like the start of a story, but nothing follows. Except Aretha Franklin and Lou Rawls and presents. He reaches into a huge blue tissue-stuffed gift bag and comes out with a soft black leather shoulder bag, topgrain Italian lambskin, a thing warm to the touch and richly fragrant. "I know how much you like black leather," his mother says very quietly.

The professor, wondering, searches her face, then kisses her cheek.

"There are two more things inside," she says.

He unzips the beautiful bag, reaches in and comes up with a black and white photo in a birds-eye maple frame: it's a picture of him as a boy in Balboa Park, San Diego, circa 1961; he's halfway up a tree, looking back at the camera and grinning, and he's wearing baggy camper shorts and a Davey Crockett coonskin cap. The professor marvels at the photo a while, admiring the amber and brown frame, and then pulls out the other gift, which is, in fact, a mint-condition 45-year-old Davey Crockett coonskin cap, bought on eBay, Mom says, for a song.

The professor balances the boy-sized cap on the top of his balding man-sized head and he pulls his mother to her feet. It's James Brown on the boom box now, and they slow-dance around the living room together just the way she taught him so many years ago, James and Mom, Please Please Please Please.

Three Weddings

1

HERE WE ARE again, Carter thinks. Junk.

Under buzzing fluorescent bulbs, with gray rain beating on the plate glass windows up front, he and his mother wander the well-worn aisles of the Goodwill. Or is it the Salvation Army? Or the VFW Bargain Basement? Carter doesn't remember and sees no reason to care. One is the same as another to him: they're all just junk stores. That's what his mother has called them all his life, not thrift stores or secondhand shops, but junk stores. Junk assails him from all sides: cast-off, stained, tattered, faded, used-up, washed out, the thousand shirts and slacks and tacky jackets on their screeching squealing wire hangers; the grubby, misshapen, scuffed-up shoes—suede chukka-boots and pebbled wingtips, velvet high heels and sling-backed pumps in faded red; the musty rows of Readers Digest Condensed Books and broken-backed novels and ancient encyclopedias missing random volumes, tomes about Nixon and the Beatles and the Korean War; and record albums, lurid splashy cover art he had long forgotten, the scratched vinyl inside harking back to pre-digital music, mechanical sound, a needle surfing a spinning groove, no wonder everything back then was groovy, he thinks; and brown-stained primitive coffee-makers and boxy toasters, clunky first-generation answering machines and the battered keyboard from an old PC, things ugly with chrome trim, smeared with fingerprints and use, things outmoded and abandoned, things usurped and replaced, things that have been around the block, that have history, that increase his sense of cluttered, squalid, unhappy lives, of life as drek. Things too sad to be kitsch. "Mom," he says—he always says—"all this junk."

"Honey," she says, "it's chaff. There are diamonds in the rough if you sift long enough. You know that."

He does know it, because she says it every time. She zones in on the diamonds; she homes like a pigeon, like radar, like vibes. He doesn't understand how she does it. He'll watch her shopping and it's as if she's guided by auras—her hand reaches out; the desired object seems to float into it; he blinks in a kind of muted amazement: again she has come up with another gem, a $200 navy blazer with the pockets still sewn shut, six bucks; an Armani dress with a tiny tear under the arm, ten dollars even; a perfectly good clock, still in the box, fifty cents because blue tags are half price on Tuesdays.

He studies his mother's face on the other side of the clothes rack. She is not quite in her middle fifties, but still beautiful, with china-doll skin, fine and unblemished; she wears her dark hair pulled back in a French braid, like a young woman; but her gray-blue wide-set eyes always seem sad to him, full of abandoned hope and resignation. Her life, he fears, has been a disappointment, one wrong turn after another, and Carter somehow understands that her junk-store sprees are partly compensation; she's bagging consolation prizes, so he is careful to chide her gently. "You're like a little girl collecting dolls that she never plays with," he'll sometimes say. "Why do you buy all this stuff? You never wear it."

"Bargains make me happy," she says. "Take happiness where you find it."

"Nobody wears polyester pants anymore."

"They're coming back in style, Jay. I read it in the paper."

"Mom, this wool blazer. Who do you know that wears a 42 long?"

She hangs it back on the nearest rack, frowning.

Last Thanksgiving in this same store Carter had barely been able to prevent her from buying a $400 plaid camel-back sofa—a steal, she'd said; all it needed was recovering, the springs were in great shape and these sofas were all the rage now, every Victorian living room had one. Carter pointed out that she had redecorated with Chinese motifs the year before, putting all her Victorian stuff in the basement. "That's because I'm ahead of the curve," she said. "Now who do we know that needs a sofa?" He couldn't believe she was about to buy this thing for no reason other than Because It's There, and he put his foot down. It did no good. She came back the next day without him and charged it.

"You are nuts, you know that?" he says now, tenderly, but his mother isn't listening. She parts the sea of frocks and blouses with one hand, and with the other, nearly in slow motion, almost hovering, she reaches and lifts a perfectly unremarkable yellow linen dress and holds it up in wonder.

"My God," she says.

"What?" Carter says.

"This dress. I don't believe it."

"What?"

"This is my wedding dress. This is the dress I wore when your father and I got married."

"You mean it's just like it?"

"No, I mean it *is* it. The exact same dress."

"No way."

"It is, Jay."

"Mom, how could it be?"

"I never thought I'd see this dress again," she says.

She doesn't look at him; she's staring at the dress. Tears stand in her eyes, and suddenly Carter realizes with a nearly physical rush of certainty—a knowledge he somehow feels is carried in his blood and bones—that she's right, this is the dress. "What in the hell is it doing here?" he says.

She had given it to the cleaning woman, years ago, when she

and Carter's dad were still married; she'd gotten rid of it one blue moody day in a fit of pique, regretful that she'd ever wed...or maybe she'd been cleaning out closets and tossing things that were dated or didn't fit anymore. She couldn't remember. All she knew was she had given it to old Bessie; Bessie had had a daughter who could wear it, she said. But how did end up here, all these years later? Carter wanted to know. His mother said she had no idea. Then she recalled that Bessie had lived nearby. "Don't you remember? We used to take her home sometimes when she missed the bus or if we needed her to stay late." So possibly that could account for why the dress was here, in this particular junk store, as opposed to one across town or even across the country.

Still, Carter thought, amazed, still, it was a miracle. It had been twenty-some years since she had given the dress away; it had been thirty-seven years last week since she had stood uneasily on her mother's lawn in that dress, clutching his father's hand and sipping a glass of punch at her hastily-arranged reception—if you could call it that. She'd always said it felt more like a wake.

She had eloped. She was already carrying Carter; she was seven weeks pregnant. It was half an hour to South Carolina, where there was no blood test, no waiting period, only a ten-dollar fee at the courthouse and a quick exchange of vows in the clerk's office. "Oh, it was quick," she says. "Of course I wanted a formal gown, you know, lots of lace and a train and a veil and everything, but we didn't have time for that, and it wouldn't have really looked right for a civil ceremony. I don't remember what your daddy wore, a dark suit, I think, probably just his church clothes, but I went down to Ivey's and got this dress the afternoon before, brand new off the rack—I think it was thirty dollars, which up to then was the most I had ever spent on a dress in my life."

Over the years, Carter has imagined the reception many times, until it has achieved a kind of snapshot clarity in his mind's eye: his mother in the yellow dress, at first contrite and then defiant, kicking off her shoes to dance barefooted in the backyard clover, in the warm late-April sun. His mother's mother frozen in a disapproving frown; her father, an old man Carter barely remembers, smiling and trying to put the best face on it. Carter's father's parents stand to one side, the mother weeping, whispering, It's all so sudden. His father's brother and his girlfriend, his mother's brother, some of the neighbors, women in housedresses and men wearing hats, that's how Carter has always envisioned them. There were no wedding photographs—no one thought to load a camera. There was no cake. They drank punch hastily improvised from ginger ale and Orange Crush, and behind the garage some of the men snuck swigs from a flask. We'll have a real reception sometime, Carter's parents promised each other; we'll have good food and music and champagne, and invite all our friends and everyone from church and we'll look them straight in the eye. Maybe after the baby's born. This was how Carter imagined it, how he thought they might feel. Of course they never had any kind of reception. They left town the next morning and set up house on the other side of the state, so his mother could endure her pregnancy free from prying eyes. In the following years he dimly remembered her wearing the yellow dress around the house and sometimes crying, for no reason he could discern. By no means was the marriage unendurable—his father was never abusive or unfaithful—but always hovering over Carter's childhood years was the feeling that his mother was bored and unhappy, that she longed for more, that she had been trapped at an early age and could not bring herself to make the best of it. And for much of his adult life, Carter, though he knew it was not his fault, had felt in some vague way responsible for his mother's unhappiness.

Now she holds the dress up for him to examine. "How much?" Carter asks.

"It's only four dollars. I'm going to get it. Since I don't have any daughters to pass it down to, I'll give it to your wife when you get married."

"Dream on," Carter says.

"Jay, you'll get married someday. That's just a fact of life." She sighs, regarding the dress wistfully at arm's length. "You know, all this dress ever brought me was bad luck. I never should have married your daddy. That was my big mistake. That's where my life jumped the tracks and I went down into the ditch."

"Thanks a lot."

"Oh, honey, I don't mean you. You know that. I'm talking about your daddy. I know there wouldn't be any you without him, but still... oh, shit."

"It's okay, Mom."

"Well," his mother says, avoiding his gaze.

"If it's bad luck, maybe you should put it back on the rack," Carter says.

"No, I want it," his mother says. "I think it'll be good to have around, to remind me how things work out. You know?"

"Then let me buy it for you," Carter says, taking the dress from her and reaching for his wallet.

"Don't be silly," his mother says.

"I'm not," he says. "I just want to. C'mon."

At last his mother smiles. "Oh, all right," she says.

At the register they're rung up by a brown-skinned crone with a wad of gum like a cud. Any moment Carter expects her to spit. She stabs at the cash register buttons and announces the total out of the side of her mouth; Carter hands her the bills and she makes change slowly with arthritic trembling hands. Carter's mother helps her fold the two shirts she's bought for her other son. The old lady strokes the linen dress as if it were angora. A smile wrinkles her face. "That's a right purty dress, Missy," she rasps.

"It's the dress I got married in," Carter's mom says.

2

"And I really think it was, man," Carter says to his brother a few days later.

"Aw, man, how could it be?" his brother says.

"If you could have seen the look on her face," Carter says.

"Well, no doubt she thinks it's the same dress. She's always off in the ozone somewhere." His brother, a dope-smoking fiend who is even then steering with his knees as he lights a bong with both hands, speaks without irony, and Carter grins behind a raised hand.

They're clattering down the two-lane in Jim's work truck. He owns both a work truck—an ancient battered blue Ford—and a play truck, what he calls the Saturday Night truck—a brand-new gleaming black Toyota that lodged, covered, in his mother's carport all week, untouched until the weekend. Out of his work truck Jim did odd jobs and landscaping; the back rattled with shovels, picks, rakes, tool-buckets, post-diggers, dusty bags of concrete mix, black plastic pots, and who knew what else, all covered with rust and red mud. "There's enough dirt in there to grow your own," Carter told Jim once, and he shook his head: "Probably is some seeds dropped back there and will be sproutin any day now."

Carter puts both feet on the dash and gives his brother a sideways glance. Jim had inherited their father's physique—lean, long-boned, big capable hands—and he has the same gray eyes as their mother with her same sad look. He'd been an unhappy baby; Carter remembers rocking him incessantly, singing to him, dangling toys before his tear-stained face and tickling his plump bare belly, but nothing seemed to work. Jim had spent his waking hours crying or moping. "I'm at the end of my rope with him, Jay-Jay," his mother would say a half-dozen times a week, or, "I'm about to tear my goddamn hair out." She swore that between his daddy and his brother she was ready to pack her bags and bail and he'd just have to do for them as best he could. Carter, caretaker, confidante, was eight at the time. Every bad day he steeled himself for the worst, but somehow she had never gotten much further than the end of the driveway. It was Carter's dad who, fed up, had finally left. His mother was relieved and then heartbroken. With both boys in the bed beside her, she'd cry herself to sleep every night. Carter wonders if his brother remembers that.

"You ought to ease up on her some, Jim," Carter says.

"Ease up, hell," Jim says. "Easy for you to say." Though Jim is past thirty, he still lives with their mother, and nearly every week there is some kind of crisis between them for Carter to adjudicate from across the state.

They pull into a grimy grocery for gas. Jim pumps while Carter heads in to pay, noting the Confederate battle flag flying over the concrete-block building. A crude stars-and-bars mural features the words "Dixie Mart" in gothic letters. Carter marvels. His brother calls from the pump, "Hey man, get me a soda," and Carter half-turns and throws him a salute. He ducks his head and steps inside over the low threshold.

To his amazement, there are two black men working the counter.

He scrounges a couple of Nehi strawberry sodas in bottles, way at the back of the case. At the register he adds two sticks of beef jerky. "And five dollars unleaded," he says. The clerks seem neither sullen nor interested. One man rings him up while the other bags solemnly.

"Look what I found," he tells Jim, back outside.

"Cool," Jim says, taking the drink. "You don't see too many Nehis anymore. You pretty much have to go out in the country to find 'em."

They drive another few miles on a twisting two-lane highway before Jim announces that he's made a wrong turn. "This place is not all that easy to find," he mutters, "and I haven't been out here for a good long while." He pulls off the blacktop and essays a three-point turn. Wary black-and-white cows gaze at them from behind barbed wire. In the next field over, the dry brown corn stalks stand abandoned. To Carter everything seems sad and washed-out in the weak winter sunlight.

"I think she's been unlucky in love, you know?" he says.

"Well, if she'd quit marrying morons, that would help," Jim says. He tears open his beef jerky with his teeth.

"Seeing her with that dress the other day, I felt sorry for her that she never had a big church wedding. I think she always wanted that."

"I was just trying to remember," Jim says, "what kind of dress she wore when she got married to Don. I ought to remember that."

"Black and gold dress, with a gold jacket," Carter says.

"Man. How did you know that? You weren't there."

"I've seen the snapshots, dude."

"Oh."

Carter had not attended his mother's second wedding. He'd been away at college, studying for his comprehensive exam; no one had even told him about it ahead of time. But he knows the photos. He kids Jim about dead brain cells and too much dope. "You stood right next to her and don't remember?"

"Man, I was sixteen years old. I didn't notice dresses back then."

"I don't think she's ever told me much about her and Don," Carter says.

"He was an asshole," Jim says. "He could have married her in a church. You know, with her and dad, they didn't really have any choice. I mean, they were on a deadline." Carter laughs. "But Don, naw, man, he just, well, he was just a dick about it the whole time. We'd been living with him two years and I think he finally married her just so she'd stop bitching about it. Did you know," Jim asks, "that on his income taxes, before they were married, he was writing her off as 'housekeeper'?"

Carter laughs. "Bet she loved that."

"Oh, man, she was livid. He'd been giving her like eight hundred bucks a month for groceries and stuff, and she found that on his taxes as a deduction for housekeeper and she hit the roof. It was nuts, you know? She was talking about turning him in to the feds. Then the next thing I know, she shows up at school one day, pulls me out of gym class to go down to the courthouse with her, and Don was there on his lunch break with his boss and his secretary, like they were the best man and the witness, whatever, and it was all over in about five minutes. They were all dressed up, you know, suits and ties and business clothes, and I was wearing jeans and torn-up sneakers. But mom wanted me there."

Carter pictures it. It should be comic, he thinks, it should be fodder for sit-coms or a story you told on yourself at a party. It is not high tragedy. Yet in his present mood it strikes him as such. He feels like weeping.

"One other thing I remember," Jim says suddenly. "That bitch woman, Don's secretary. We went to this swanky restaurant afterwards and she threw a fit over their hearts of palm salad. She kept saying how 'divine' it was, and how she 'adored' hearts of palm, and I didn't know what the hell she was talking about. I looked over at Mom, and all of a sudden I saw that she didn't know what it was either. She'd never had it, and it was just...man...it just sucked. It was like this pompous bitch just had to do something to put mom in her place, like she was so refined and mom was just an ignorant little hillbilly." Jim shakes his head. "You know why I remember that?"

"Why?"

" 'Cause two years ago Mom took me out on my birthday to a place that had hearts of palm salad, and she ordered it. And she didn't like it. She told me she'd been waiting all that time just to see what it was like, and now she knew, and it wasn't anything like what she thought it would be."

"Christ," Carter says. "What a sad frigging story."

"Naw, man, it ain't sad. She finally got to put that thing to rest. She'd been obsessing about that hearts of palm for fifteen years."

Carter sees his mother and brother in a candlelit restaurant holding salad forks. He sees his mother in jeans and tee-shirt with a yellow dress folded over her arm. He sees his dad with a .22 rifle at the top of the stairs and some boyfriend of his mother's at the door below and his mother standing between them with his dad yelling for her to get out of the way and he and Jim, children, trying to hold his father back. I could weep, he thinks; I could actually cry real tears right now. What's wrong with me?

"Jay, you worry too much," his brother says.

"It just seems so sad to me." Carter looks blankly out the window.

"Things seem to be one thing, but maybe they're something else," Jim explains. "And in the meantime," he says, downshifting, "here we are." He turns into a dirt parking lot by a bright red-and-white sign: HOYLE'S U-PULL-IT JUNKYARD.

3

"HEY, MR. HOYLE," Jim says as Carter follows him inside.

An old man in greasy overalls tells them hey. "What you fellas need?" he asks.

Lifters is what they need, Jim explains, lifters for the hatchback of their mother's Honda.

"Hatch won't stay up?" old man Hoyle asks, and Jim nods. "Thing'll fall shut and chop off ye head, will it?"

"That's about it," Carter tells him. He has a bruise at the base of his skull to prove it.

"Things get wore out, boys," Hoyle explains. "Ever last thing on God's earth." Squinting at Carter, he asks the year of their mother's car.

"Eighty-nine Honda Civic hatchback."

After a moment's reflection, Hoyle reckons he's got maybe two dozen of those. Most pretty picked over, though. All the way to the back, second to last row, he tells them. "Got ye metric socket? Lifters is ten bucks apiece. Run you thirty-five or forty new, so that's a deal."

"Thanks, Mr. Hoyle." Jim leads Carter out into the junkyard. They pass a sign that reads ENTER @ YR OWN RISK. The old man calls after them and they turn. He laughs. "Watch out ye don't drop the hatch on ye head once ye get them lifters off."

Carter waves him an okay. "Man," he tells his brother, "I'd hate to pay the liability insurance on this place."

"I doubt seriously he's got any insurance," Jim says.

They wander among the wrecked cars, Carter thinking about his mother's third wedding.

For some years after she had left Don—moving out in the middle of the night, Carter and Jim loading her furniture while Don slept—she had not dated at all. She told Carter she had given up on men. They were liars, cheats, not to be trusted; they brought nothing but misery. She didn't need a man in her life; she could be strong and happy on her own. Then she met Gene in a 24-hour Stop Shop. He was standing, hungover and lost, in front of an endcap display of cases of beer. "He looked so pathetic," his mother said later, "he looked like a little stray dog somebody had been kicking," and though Carter had never known his mother to take in strays, there was something else about this man, with his haunted blue eyes and unkempt hair. He reminded her of someone—exactly who, she couldn't say—and then she could. Her father had sometimes had that same look. "My heart just melted," she told Carter. "I was stupid. I couldn't see straight. I suppose I thought the third time was a charm." She bought him a twelve-pack and took him home and they drank it together. For the next year she bought his beer and drove him around—his license had been permanently revoked—cooked for him and occasionally paid his overdue child support to keep him out of jail. Carter and his brother hated Gene. To his face, Jim called him a pathetic blood-sucking leech and a scumbag, and Carter stopped visiting home altogether.

"It was a big lifestyle change," his mother had admitted later. She wasn't used to alcohol, not regularly or in volume, but at Gene's insistence, she drank to keep him company. One night, drunk, they'd gotten married in the same convenience store where they'd met. Gene had a buddy who worked there on the graveyard shift, a fellow AA dropout who had once been an ordained Full Gospel preacher. Usually he did not marry people who'd been drinking, he told them, but Gene was a buddy and had slipped him $50 to boot, so he'd made an exception. No forms were filed, no rings exchanged, just a recitation of vows, a kiss, and an extended prayer to bless the union. " 'God does not require a piece of paper in a file-cabinet at the courthouse'," Carter's mom quoted the preacher as saying; " 'You stand here as man and wife in the eyes of God and that is all that is required and let no man put asunder, amen'." When Carter had heard the news, he'd insisted that the marriage had not been legal, that since there was no record of it, it was not binding, but his mother didn't care; whether or not it was a marriage, she said, it had been a wedding. In jeans, a teal sweatshirt, and tennis shoes, she had stood before God and witnesses—a high school girl buying cigarettes and the other cashier—and declared that she would love and honor and obey till death did them part, so there. Carter could not talk sense to her; she was beyond logic, he saw, so he let it go, and he shook Gene's hand and unhappily welcomed him to the family.

It hadn't lasted long. One day Carter's mom came home to find his closet cleaned out and her jewelry box missing. The note on the kitchen table said only that he was sorry and he'd call in a few days. The next time she'd heard from him was a week later, and he was in Utah, drunk. He called again, twice more over the next month, and after that she had heard nothing. In another few days it would be three years since she'd seen him.

Good riddance, Carter thinks now. Lowlife. Better that she be miserable without him than dragged down with him.

He and his brother head uphill past Fords and Chevys, Dodges and AMCs. "They *would* put the Hondas at the back," Jim says. Carter grunts. Everywhere he looks, sunlight bounces from chrome and glass, like a thousand tiny flares exploding one after another. They pass a dozen trucks of the same make as his brother's, several twisted and smashed horribly. There's a wrecked row of red Toyotas like their father's, and then a line of British sports cars. Carter, who had once owned an MG, shudders. "This is damned creepy," he says. He has never seen so much twisted metal, such blatant records of violent impact. He watches a hogsnake slide under a yellow Jaguar.

When they finally reach the Honda section, Carter stops at the first hatchback. "That's not an '89," Jim tells him; "see, the taillights are the wrong shape." He points. "There's one."

They stand before a blue Civic that doubtless once had been identical to their mother's, but now is crusted with rust and missing a passenger door. Dockweed grows around the flattened tires. "Pop the hatch," Jim says, peering in through the back window, socket wrench in hand.

Carter opens the driver's door and gropes on the floor for the hatch release. The last driver of this car, he noticed, had hit the windshield hard; over the crumpled steering wheel the safety glass is fractured like an unbroken puzzle. Looking around the familiar black and gray interior, he cannot prevent himself from envisioning his mother's death.

It's not fair, he thinks, holding up the hatch as Jim ratchets the lifters loose. She didn't deserve this life, this tapestry of loneliness and disappointment. He realizes he's thinking childishly; he doesn't care. It would have been a simple thing to make her happy.

"What's wrong?" his brother asks, looking at him.

"I feel like we ought to say a prayer," he says, "for whoever drove this car last."

But Carter is not a praying man. Nor is it the unknown driver he finds himself invoking. Instead, he imagines a wedding. He gives the bride a dazzling white dress, lace and crinoline and a veil and white slippers. He gives her a candlelit church, pews lined with happy, approving friends and family. He makes the mother of the bride, in lavender, beam from the front row; he places the father in the aisle in a gray tuxedo. Carter shapes a groom, tall and good and kind, waiting faithfully beside the altar. And he puts himself and his brother there too, in tuxes, both weeping small happy tears, weeping with joy for their mother. And this is what I would do, Carter whispers to himself, just this, if only I could. Amen.

Siam Spoon Sushi

IT WAS NOT until the fourth year of the twenty-first century that Thai food came to our town, and when it did, it came as two separate restaurants opening within a month of each other. The first carried the prosaic name of the Bangkok Cafe and elicited from wags and the hoi-polloi a predictable series of vulgar puns and sexual innuendoes, sometimes accompanied by pelvic thrusts or moans of mock passion. The other restaurant was called something none of us could understand—"Siam Spoon Sushi"—a name that may have been melodious or meaningful in the Thai language, but in English seemed some sort of non sequitur.

But we were willing—we who had traveled, who had eaten in bistros and boarding houses and bars and dives and four-star restaurants all over the world—to overlook the odd names, for the indigenous cooking of our region is based on a regimen of fatback and fast-food and fried-to-death everything, a few pizza places and a Chinese buffet, and we longed and prayed and hungered for something—anything—more exotic. The Siam Spoon Sushi featured not only the usual curry and noodle dishes made with lemongrass and basil and the fiery Thai peppers, but also for a month or two offered the most extensive menu of sushi in town, and even a selection of Laotian dishes such as larp and sticky rice. So great was our need for the exotic, the uncommon, that it seemed for a while that our small town would be able to support both restaurants, and that people were about evenly divided on which to patronize, for though Siam Spoon Sushi had a more extensive menu, The Bangkok Cafe was less expensive and had better feng shui. Differences of opinion aside, all agreed that having two Thai restaurants was better than having one, and we'd have been grateful just to have one.

For our crowd the Siam Spoon Sushi held a slight edge. The menu was funnier ("We Can Alter The Spicy According To Your Taste"; "It Is Worht Having Thai Food"; etc.). It was on our side of town, and was a little funkier, darker inside and a little more run-down, which we liked. It was not uncommon for us to eat there twice a week, or even more: Marianne mentioned proudly one night over her Pad Thai that she'd been there for lunch already that day.

But then things started to go wrong.

The young Asian man who ran the Siam Spoon Sushi claimed his name was Frank and he was from Milwaukee, though the quality of his English indicated he was not a native speaker. Frank came in as manager a few months after the restaurant opened, and his smiling, blissfully inattentive look seemed to infect the whole staff. Younger people were hired. Soon a hand-lettered NO SUSHI sign appeared in the window over the Siam Spoon Sushi sign; "Chef have quit, no more sushi," was all we could get out of Frank. "Are you going to hire someone else?" one of us asked, and Frank just lifted his shoulders as if it were folly to try, as if sushi chefs were rare as diamonds and temperamental as opera stars, and what kind of Thai restaurant served Japanese food anyway? A week later, a friend of ours picking up a late-night order swore he'd seen the Laotian waitress shimmying to Madonna tunes atop the defunct sushi bar. We began to notice an increasing frequency of garble between table and kitchen—we'd end up with green curry chicken instead of shrimp, or a bowl of coconut soup instead of Thai iced tea. The sanitation rating dropped to a very high "B." We started to wonder what these people were on. Still, we hung in there, because eating at The Spoon was an adventure and half the ambiance of the place came from the fuckups.

One night two of us went in for takeout: Drunken Noodles

with Tofu, vegetarian spring rolls, mango rice. Instead of the usual Southeast Asian music videos, this particular night Frank's wide-screen TV was showing a Thailand travelogue, and we watched a Caucasian tourist sitting down to dinner in a hut with a toothless brown Thai man. With chopsticks—not spoons—they began chowing down on something that looked like fried grasshoppers or grubs or cicadas. Frank, handing us our change, apparently noticed our expressions, because he said with a note of wounded surprise, "They are very good!" "Insects?" we asked doubtfully. "Yes! Very good!" "Just the idea of it," Jessica said, and shuddered. "But even Americans can eat them," Frank explained; "they taste just like…." He stared at us doubtfully, struggling to find a word that perhaps does not exist in English. Finally he blurted out with great earnestness: "They are not poisonous!"

We said we were very happy they were not poisonous.

THE NEXT WEEK all six of pulled up for dinner at the Siam Spoon Sushi and found the place locked and dark, a CLOSED sign taped above the NO SUSHI sign. Despair, groans, gnashing of teeth, tearing of hair. "Damn him," one of us said. "Dumbass," another said. We piled back into our autos and caravanned across town to the Bangkok Cafe, cursing to each other via cell phone, or staring glumly out the car windows.

At the Bangkok our demeanor was mournful and our chatter was muted. We ordered a tableful of food—Phad Prik Moo, Maeng Masaman Nuer, Panang Gung, Pla Tod—and dug in. Unlike Siam Spoon Sushi, where Frank cranked at high volume some sort of Asian Industrial Death Metal, the Bangkok Cafe exuded tranquility and tastefulness. A murmuring water fountain on a tripod table trickled at the front door, and ambient music played from the ceiling speakers—lute-like stringed things, gongs, windchimes, an occasional soft clap of wood blocks. The tiny waitresses wore sarongs, not tight jeans and tank tops, and their every gesture was delicate and elegant; and they were managed with great formality by "Your Owner and Hostess Alak Niratpattanasai." The food, we had to admit, was excellent.

After the last of our party had pushed back his plate, one of us beckoned Ms. Niratpattanasai over and asked what had happened to her competitor. She narrowed her eyes and said in clipped English that Frank was a fool. Perhaps we did not know, she said, that she herself had been owner of both restaurants, and that the boy who called himself Frank was her own nephew, and she had watched this very bad boy destroy all she had accomplished with the Siam Spoon Sushi, and therefore because of this in addition he would never again manage any of her restaurants, for he was a boy of great badness. But out of respect for her dead sister, the boy's mother, she said, she would not allow him to live on the street where he deserved. "He is dishwasher now," she said. "All of these dishes," and she indicated with a sweep of her hand the whole restaurant. She turned then, dignified and haughty, and left to check on another table.

"Holy shit," one of us said.

No one wanted dessert after that. But as we were gathering our things, purses and car keys and cell phones, and passing around the bill and calculating the tip, dessert came: five bowls of green tea ice cream, each garnished with a maraschino cherry, and one order of mango rice for the vegan in our party. "We didn't order th—" one of us started to say, and our waitress raised one finger to her lips and motioned with her eyes toward the kitchen. In the steamy round window of the kitchen door we could see Frank's face, though we could not read his expression. He gazed at us a moment, then very slowly bowed his head and backed away.

Our waitress leaned toward us. "Frank say You eat sweet," she said softly. "Eat before sweet melt."

So we did.

In the Hurricane

Gene Weaver

THE DAY AFTER the worst hurricane in living memory, Gene Weaver cuts figure-eights in the street on his trick bike, bumping over debris and downed pecan branches and dead power lines. Gene Weaver must be sixty, but he rides a twelve-year-old's bike: banana seat, sissy bar, butterfly grips; and he's contrived to wrap part of a faded blue bumpersticker around his handlebars: AGE NOT HAT. He wears thrift-store teeshirts and shorts and black wingtips. Black hair grows from his craggy red nose. He is a retard, people say, and a drunk off and on the wagon. Drunks in our town get DWIs and lose their licenses but some of them keep driving anyway. Others sidestep the law on alkie bikes—mopeds or scooters. But Gene Weaver sticks with his trick bike, though his only trick is to swoop in wobbly circles and figure-eights while declaiming in a loud voice about the blesséd Holy Spirit. Also he can make a sound like a police siren.

Gene Weaver at one time was my friend, but much has changed in 24 hours. His slick tires cut along the curb-edge, and now and again he shakes his fist at our porch. I go out to see what he wants.

"A worser person than a axe-murderer," he says.

"Hey, Gene Weaver," I say.

"To open the bolted door to a whore-mongering child of Ham, like he was the verily prodigal son himself."

"Where did you hear that?" I say.

"Pitchers have little ears," he says. "You ourt to be in the jail."

I watch him bump over a branch. He teeters, then catches himself.

"There is a judgment and a lein," he announces. "It is foretold."

In this context I don't even know what a lein is and I tell him so. He ignores me, probably because he doesn't know either.

"You kilt the fatted calf for him," Gene Weaver says. "Yet was I afire, you'd not even piss on me. Was I afflicted, you'd not even render me a cloak."

He stops the bike, straddles it, and shakes his fist at the house again, staring a bit above my head. In another minute I half-expect to see him foaming at the mouth. I tell him cloaks can't heal afflictions.

"You and your brood is spawn of the devil," Gene Weaver hisses. He pops a pecan shell under his tire, then rides off scowling.

Accent

I AM NEW here, and am still studying the accent. The word "house" is pronounced as "hice" (rhymes with "nice"). The word "out" is pronounced as "oat," like the narrator on *The Waltons*. So you might hear Gene Weaver explain that when he was young and poor his family "had to take our shites in the oat-hice." Schoolchildren taught to "sound it out" spell *town* as *tine*, *county* as *kinety*. The word "fish" is pronounced "feesh," and no outsider can hear the difference between "herring" and "heron."

On the second or maybe third day after the hurricane, when the sheriff drives by and we're sitting on the porch after curfew, he backs up and calls over his loudspeaker, "Y'all get on in the hice." We stand up and turn and he drives off and then we sit down again. Jerome says, "He could have just as easy cracked his winda and talk to us like we human beans, but not this sheriff." Jerome tosses a pecan backhanded into the street. "This sheriff always got to be busting your balls 'bout something."

Jerome

JEROME IS OUR black man. You cannot really call him our African-American man unless you are an idiot or are making mock. Miss Deedee next door calls Jerome her nigra man, but never to his face. He belongs to most of the hices on this block, in that he does the yardwork whether you want him to or not. You leave one morning and when you come back for lunch the grass is magically cut and leaves raked up, and around supper that night or a few nights later Jerome will knock on the door and ask to be paid. Occasionally he will ask to be paid before he cuts the grass, sometimes a week in advance, and some people agree to that some of the time, and some don't most of the time, and quickly the accounts get jumbled and no one knows how far ahead or far behind they stand with Jerome. Once he was in jail for two weeks and as Miss Deedee said the neighborhood started looking like something out of nigratown. If you are an old lady, Jerome calls you "ma'am" or "Miss Deedee" or "Miss Sally," and if you are an old man he calls you "Suh" or "Cap'n" as if he's a living relic from a Faulkner story, but if you're young and hip he'll call you "homes" or "sistah." If you are Gene Weaver, he doesn't speak Word One.

Hurricane

WE WAITED A week for the hurricane—they were tracking it that long or longer—and when it came in we had nailed up and battened down and X-ed out with masking tape and stocked up on batteries and bottled water and everything else, so when it got here, there was nothing to do but sit on the porch and watch the trees going down all around us.

The porch of our house was in the lee of the wind, so as stupid as it sounds, we sat out on the buckled paint-peeled floorboards and smoked a little weed right there on Oakum Street and looked at each other and yelled If the wind shifts we're going to have to go inside.

And down the sidewalk came Jerome, holding his do-rag hat clamped to his head. The rain was horizontal and he was tap-dancing over the sparking loops and coils of downed power lines. "Jerome!" we screamed. "Get your crazy ass up here on this porch this instant." Jerome looked up, made big ju-ju eyes at us like a darkie in an old racist movie, and started laughing. "I wouldn't be callin' nobody a crazy ass," he hollered over the wind, "if I was smokin dope in broad daylight on Oakum Street."

He hopped up the three stairs, shook water like a big dog, and reached for the joint.

And so that's how Jerome came to ride out the storm with us on our front porch, and after, to sleep on our sofa.

How he had come to be walking down the street in a hurricane was like this, he said: One time he was visiting a fine foxy lady friend in St. Louis, Missouri, and on the radio he heard that the temperature was 3 degrees and the wind was blowing 30 miles an hour and so the wind chill added up to 18 below zero, and he thought, Nobody in my family all the way back to Africa has ever been out in weather 18 below zero, and so he decided he would walk around the block just so he could tell 'em about it later. So he did. The snot froze in his nose, he says, and the air was like an ice knife stabbing his lungs, but later he was glad he'd done it; it was amazing. He paused, and then, in case we didn't get it, he said that nobody in his family had ever been out in a hurricane either.

"Jerome, that's insane," Diana said.

The true reason he was out in a hurricane, we found out later, was that his mama had kicked him out again. For good this time.

"You're liable to get electrocuted," I said, waving the back of my hand at the sparking power lines.

"Naw," Jerome said, passing the joint back. "Just like playin hopscotch."

We stood up to watch a huge old pecan in our front yard teeter, teeter, then with a hideous noise uproot itself and crash across the street and through the roof of our neighbor's house.

"Ah ha ha ha ha ha ha!" Jerome howled.

"Hey, man, that's not funny."

"Ah ha ha ha!"

"What's so funny?"

"Ah hee hee ha! Ah hee hee ha!" Jerome has this laugh, you have to hear it in person sometime. Finally he was able to explain that the tree had just gone through the roof of the house of Gene Weaver's uncle.

"Up there in that attic," he said, "do you know what's in there?"

"No."

"Boxes and boxes of pitchers of Gene Weaver when he was little. Photo albums full of that motherfucker. And you see that hole in the roof there? Do you know what's happenin right now to all them pitchers? Ah ha ha hee!"

Churches

IN TOWN WE have seven churches: two Baptist, one Methodist, one African Methodist Episcopal Zion, a Catholic that offers two services, one in English and one in Spanish, a Church of Christ, and a Pentecostal Holiness. In the county there are exactly twice as many churches, but less variety: mostly all Baptist and Pentecostal.

A self-ordained preacher holds services in his garage, and at one of the crossroads sits an abandoned Temple of the Holy Ghost Meeting House, a kudzu riot showing through the broken-out stained glass windows. It was twenty-eight years ago this spring when Gene Weaver's father Bud had his heart attack at the pulpit, and that was the last service ever preached there, unless you count the times that Gene played preacher to a congregation of squirrels and rat snakes, field mice and quail.

Diana says, "Until the day he died, Bud Weaver would look you right square in the eye and a propos of nothing say, 'August twenty-second, nineteen and seventy-one. The worst day in the history of Aldon County'."

The day the schools desegregated.

Sheriff

IN OUR TOWN the sheriff is black and the chief of police is white. Things seem to work out okay that way.

The third day after the hurricane our street is still without power and the black sheriff stops by to see if he wants us to arrest Jerome.

"Is he botherin' y'all?" the sheriff wants to know. "If he is, I can take him off your hands."

"How did you even know he was here?" I ask.

"I like to keep my eye on him. I purdy much know where he is most of the time."

Diana is wearing a pair of yellow gym shorts and a tank top without a bra—her pajamas, in other words. You can tell the sheriff is impressed with her, because he looks everywhere but.

"How's your daddy doin," he finally asks Diana.

"Still just as mean as ever," she says.

They go to the same church, she tells me later, so the sheriff has seen her daddy more recently than she has.

Jerome is no trouble, we say to the sheriff. We tell him that we're sure he has more important things to be doing, what with the town under curfew and the TV vulture-people feeding frenzy and the M-16-toting National Guard careening around in their dumbass Humvees. Except we don't say "dumbass Humvees."

Even so, the sheriff tells us it's better not to get the smart-mouth with law enforcement. He climbs back into his car and scrawls something on his clipboard, then kills the blue light and rolls off.

Jerome's Secrets

How is Jerome able to nap anytime, anywhere, at the slightest notice? "Keep your eyes sleepy."

What is the best way to cook Miss Deedee's thawed freezer full of chicken breasts, all at once? "Get some of these fallen-down pee-can branches and build us a fire in the backyard. Brush on some hot pepper vinegar and sugar and a little oregano and my secret spice. Cook 'til they done, then put on rubber gloves and tear the meat off the bone and thow it in a big bowl. Call the neighbors."

Why did Jerome paint his rake and hoe and wheelbarrow and even his ancient chuffing lawnmower pink? " 'Cause won't nobody be stealin no pink rake, homes. Except maybe faggots. Ah ha hee hee ha."

History

Not long after Diana had left her boyfriend and moved in with me, we were in bed one night and I asked her to tell me about Gene Weaver.

"Gene Weaver," she said, and sniffed. She seemed to drift for a while. Then she said, "I've known Gene Weaver nearly all my life. He was always underfoot. I remember Gene Weaver better than I remember my own grandma."

"Is that why you don't like him?" I say.

"I never said I didn't like him."

"Okay."

I waited but she said nothing else. So I asked her flat-out what was the story, why were Gene Weaver and Jerome like poison to each other?

"I guess from church," Diana said after a while. "Which is one reason I stay away from *that* bullshit."

Back in the day, half the white churches preached integration, and half didn't. All the black churches were for it. On Broad Street one Sunday afternoon Gene Weaver's daddy flung a vanilla ice cream cone in the face of the A.M.E. Zion preacher, Reverend Percival T. Johnston, and then he threw a punch. Reverend Johnston turned the other cheek but some of his people did not. "It was a full-fledged race-riot here for a few days. We had the Klan come in on one side and the NAACP on the other. Half the white churches were passing out HERITAGE NOT HATE bumper-stickers and flying the Stars & Bars, and the other half was peeling off the bumper-stickers and tearing down the flag." Federal marshals were called in, and the schools desegregated.

"I still don't understand," I said. "All this was decades ago, right?"

Diana zoned out; it looked like she was counting cracks in the ceiling. Her mouth was moving, but no sound. Finally she said, "When you put a bunch of white kids and black kids together… some of them hate each other…some of them don't care one way or another…. But a few of them fall in love."

Diana's mother was the first white girl in her school to openly date a black boy. The boy was Jerome's father.

"No friggin' way," I said.

"Small town, babe." She closed her eyes. "They didn't date long and they didn't stay friends after, but that didn't matter." Months after the breakup Bud Weaver and some of his crew bumped into Jerome's father on the street and they beat the daylights out of him; once he was down, they kicked him until balled up like a baby and rolled into the gutter, begging and crying. "Bud and them were charged with assault and some other things, and right after that was when Bud had his heart attack. He was out on bail at the time."

Diana turned over on her tummy and rested her chin on a pillow. "They put the rest of them on trial but it was a fucked-up bunch of rednecks on the jury and everybody was acquitted."

"And Jerome's dad?"

"Left town right after and nobody has heard squat from him in thirty-some years."

"Jesus," I said.

"History lesson over," Diana said. She turned her head flat against the pillow, facing away from me. "P.S.," she said quietly, "my daddy was one of the ones acquitted."

ABC Store

You CAN GET wine and beer at the Piggly Wiggly as long as you're buying any day except Sunday before 1 P.M., but if you want a bottle of whiskey you've got to get it at Aunt Betty's Cafe, which is what Jerome calls the Alcoholic Beverage Control store. After the storm, there's a dusk-to-dawn curfew and the ABC store is locked down tight, but despite the National Guard being bivouacked across the parking lot, someone puts a cinderblock through the plateglass and grabs a few half-gallon plastic jugs of Popov vodka and some RonRico rum before they burn rubber out of there.

Even though Jerome doesn't have a car, the sheriff thinks he might have something to do with it. That's what we figure out later, after his second visit.

Eight days after the storm, power is back on in eighty percent of town and they lift the curfew and reopen the ABC and there is a run on anything that will make you feel good, a line out the door of lawyers' wives and good ol' boys and relief workers and street folk and TV reporters and teachers with too much time on their hands. Everybody is extra happy to be getting their hooch, and they smile and hug and tell hurricane stories. And later that night in our neighborhood people gather on the curbs and sidewalks to pass bottles and make merry, laughing and hooting and calling *whooooooo-eee!* and yelling things to each other like "Give me back my motherfuckin pie!" and "Darlene a crackhead!" and after a few hours of this, they begin fighting. Diana and I hear them screaming at each other and then at the cops, and we hear the cops ordering them to disperse over their P.A.'s and we hear more cops coming up with the sirens going and people screaming Run, run! I say that Jerome will probably be spending the night in jail tonight, but about 2:15 everything gets quiet except for the goddamn vowel-barking dog—Rah! Reh! Rih! Roo! Roo! over and over again—and then around 3:30 A.M. we hear Jerome easing in our back door, and when we get up in the morning he's splayed on the sofa with his shoes on and an empty half-pint bottle of Pepe Lopez tequilla in one hand.

Sexual Energy

"ARE YOU SURE there isn't some sexual energy between you and Jerome?" I find myself asking on the third day after the storm.

"There's sexual energy everywhere," is all Diana will say.

Smoking dope always makes me sleepy and I crash early. Diana and Jerome hang in the candlelit living room with their faces turned toward the dead blank screen of the TV, passing back and forth a big bag of Fritos. I can hear them laughing in my sleep.

Miss Deedee heats a huge stockpot of hot water over the firepit Jerome dug in her backyard and she ladles us some into a couple of old plaid thermoses so that we can take a sponge bath. Diana stands in her sockfeet with her panties around her ankles and lets me wash her all over. I take my time and later she returns the favor.

We bump into Diana's gynecologist on the street. There are only two gynecologists in town and this is the young good-looking one; he's wearing a bicycle helmet and shorts and he's unshaven. He says he's pulled two consecutive 18-hour shifts at the ER and he's starting to hallucinate. He's in a fugue state, he says. You have to wonder what it's like to be on intimate terms with half the twats in town.

The All Star Dance School usually lets out every Tuesday and Thursday afternoon at 5 P.M. and for a few minutes the street in front of our house is filled with little girls in tutus and older girls in jazz and tap outfits and a few high school girls, the teacher assistants, in their tight leotards with their bare midriffs showing pierced belly-buttons. Since the hurricane there haven't been any dance lessons or any dancers.

One time Gene Weaver tried to feel up an eight-year-old girl but her daddy dropped the charges after the Chief of Police explained that Gene Weaver was doing what any normal ten-year-old boy would do. At the time Gene Weaver was in his late forties.

Advice from Gene Weaver

"THERE IS A lot of drugs in the schools and my advice to anyone is to avoid school."

"When the Commander says 'Jump,' you better jump."

"Noah's son Ham saw his daddy naked. From that, he got the boot. God sent him to Africa and burned his skin black. The sons and daughters of Ham is still with us today. Best thing to do is not mess with what God has set aside."

Various Things Happen

TREES ARE DOWN all over town: hundred-year-old oaks, eighty-foot tall pecans and maples. There's a tulip tree on my truck. Our street is blocked one way by a giant sycamore, the other by broken pavement and downed power poles. If you want out you can drive across Miss Deedee's front yard and bump down the curb. Some guys come by with chainsaws and try to cut through the sycamore but the saws are too small. On the fourth day a big front-loader spends half the morning tugging the tree aside. Once our street is reopened, Diana's old boyfriend drives by about twice a day, gawking out his window at our house.

The vacant field by our airstrip is the dropoff point for downed trees and branches. They have three chippers going 24 hours a day, and trucks from five counties away hauling off the chips.

The Lions Club and the Optimists crank their portable gas grills at the high school and get the word out that they'll cook anything anyone brings them. Don't let your thawed food go to waste. An orgy of eating ensues. People knocking on doors, giving away extra pork chops and the like.

Free bags of ice at the Piggly-Wiggly: stand in line at the refrigerator truck.

The National Guard hands out bottled water and the Red Cross hands out bottled water and candles and matches and tampons and diapers and batteries for radios.

Into town come the Texas Baptist Men in their tool-laden vans. They start reshingling roofs right away.

Diana's old boyfriend sits on the green bench in front of the drugstore with his Martin acoustic guitar and plays and sings a not-very-good song about the hurricane that he says he wrote during the hurricane. "While we were in the eye, actually," he says. Like that somehow makes it a good song or something.

The Government

THE GOVERNMENT SENDS around some people door to door to see how everybody's making out. Ours is a little bald white man wearing khaki shorts and mirrored wrap-around sunglasses that make him look like an alien robot. "What do y'all need?" he says, and he writes the answers down.

Miss Deedee says, "Lord honey I don't need a thing. Just some help getting these sticks and branches up out my yard."

Diana says, "Some electricity would be nice. I'd like to wash some clothes. I'm out of clean underwear."

I say, "Is the water still okay to drink? Ours looks a little brown."

Jerome says, "I'll tell you what we need. I'll say it real slow so you can spell it." And then he spells, one letter at a time, "M-O-R-E   M-A-R-Y-W-A-N-N-A."

Everything is Changed

THE MYSTICAL POWER of natural phenomena. Once I had a Spanish teacher who had been in Costa Rica for a total eclipse of the sun. It was spiritual, she said. The whole country turned out and watched. At totality, the firey corona shot out around the dark disk, followed by winking diamond shapes. Dogs howled and roosters crowed, greeting the imagined new day. "Everything is changed after that," she said. "The whole world. Here, in my heart. Everywhere. Nothing could be the same."

That's how the mayor wants to spin the hurricane. The situation is bad but there's nowhere to go but up, he says on the local Christian radio show, and we can make this a new beginning. "Our town has suffered adversity before," he says. "Negative press, divisiveness. But all that's over now. All over town I see us coming together, neighbor to neighbor, lending helping hands, chainsaws, clean water. This storm has changed everything."

"Maybe now he'll get that new Walmart he's been wanting," Diana says, and with her thumb and index finger she lifts the transister radio by its wrist strap like picking up a rat by its tail and drops it in the trash bucket.

Jerome moves out.

Recovery

THE MONTH AFTER the hurricane, Diana's old boyfriend asks her to sing with his shitkicker band one more time, for a good cause, he points out, at the Hurricane Recovery Celebration Festival. Diana squeezes into her sequined white jumpsuit and then covers half of it with a jeans jacket. "I can't believe I used to wear this shit," she says to me right before going onstage. She sings harmony with her eyes closed and she won't smile at anyone, but Donald gives her a sideways hug when she's done and won't let her off without an encore.

There's a parade later in which the mayor rides his motorcycle and the high school band plays "I Will Survive" and "Rock Around the Clock," the tubas grunting between notes. From the bed of a white pickup truck covered with cotton-ball clouds, the choir director of the First Pentecostal Church waves and beckons: he's dressed as Jesus—white robe, wig, Birkenstocks. Behind the firetrucks, howling like a siren, comes Gene Weaver on his trick bike, cutting figure eights and pelting us bystanders with hard red candy. People wave and call his name and tease him and hoot and pretty girls blow him kisses. He has nothing to say to anyone; he just howls louder.

And coming up the rear, after the Lazy Z Horse Stable Equestrian Team, is Jerome. He's wearing a pair of black nylon sweatpants and a black windbreaker, shouldering his pink rake, and he's drunk. He's drunk and unauthorized, running from one fresh pile of horseshit to another and scraping it steaming into the gutter with the steel tines of the rake making a hideous metallic sound on the asphalt, and he's rolling his wild eyes and laughing at us all: Ah ha ha hee hee!

How to Build a House

A cap is the first thing you need, preferably a primary color, emblazoned with the logo of a tool company or a lumberyard—Snap-On, DeWalt, Remo, Plum Creek, Georgia Pacific—or a common brand of beer or perhaps a hot sauce—Tabasco, Texas Pete, Hot Cock Vietnam. Avoid mauve or chartreuse caps featuring yacht club names or internet service provider logos. Note also that although its correct name is "cap," no one calls it "cap"; here, in the circles you move in, it is a "hat." The second thing you will need is a truck, preferably a Ford, Chevy, or Dodge. A Japanese truck counts, but not much.

Draw every stick of lumber, every brick, every nail, every strip of aluminum flashing, every bead of glue on each tongue-in-groove panel of plywood; draw in hyper-realistic enlarged detail; draw in colored pencils with coded colors for each material and construction sequence. Draw draw draw. Tell yourself: *If you can draw it, you can build it.* Delay breaking ground until you have finished the drawings, all of the drawings. Keep drawing long enough and you might not have to build it.

Get back to nature. Find a waterfront building site on a beautiful tea-colored river eleven miles from the closest town, forty-two miles from a secular bookstore or an iced latte, two counties away from the nearest daily newspaper, a site where the display screen of your cellphone blinks NO SERVICE AVAILABLE. Drive a few stakes under the cypress trees and string some line. Start digging. A few weeks after you've finished the foundation, get married to a local woman with two teenagers. Your two favorite rooms in the house—your study and your music room—are now morphed in an instant into teenage bedrooms. You stand where your built-in birds-eye maple desk was going to be and look out over the tea-colored river and you think *surfboards, stuffed animals, Brittany Spears posters.*

THE LAST TIME your wife ventured out to help you on the house you took her up on the roof with a 3000-count plastic bucket of button-cap nails and three rolls of 30-pound roofing felt; the two of you rolled out the long black strips of felt, overlapping the seams and nailing them down every six inches. Your wife, squatting on the hot roof with Little Tap-Tap, says the nails' orange plastic heads on the black tarpaper remind her of Halloween, as if these precise rows of nails were cute little pumpkins lined up like soldiers. You watch her bend a nail, pull it out and toss it over her shoulder, start another one and bend it, start a third and smack it sideways so that it ricochets off into the woods. Easy, you tell her, these are expensive. She reproaches you by hammering in the next dozen perfectly. You got it now, you say, but she just gives you a look. You turn for another handful of nails and accidentally kick the 3000-count bucket with the side of your workboot and watch it tilt and tip and spew two-thousand-nine-hundred-and-sixty-seven nails across the ridge and down the steep plywood sheathing, a rushing flood of airborne orange nails headed over the eve, a stormburst of orange raindrops pelting your backyard.

WHEN YOU CAN'T stand the sawdust and dirt on your plywood subfloor another single day, get in your Japanese truck and make a special trip to Beldon's Welding and Hardware to buy a broom.

There is a very pretty young woman in Beldon's who can distinguish at a glance a half-inch lag screw from a five-eights inch lag screw, who coifs her brown hair in a loose swirl held in place with a couple of 16-penny nails, who wears bluejean shorts and tennis shoes and a chartreuse Beldon's Welding teeshirt and has brown arms and legs in the dead of winter and level brown eyes, and just for fun you have a desultory crush on her and think of her as your Secret Girlfriend. You always contrive to check out when she is manning the rickety old cash register, and today she looks at you holding this broom, an ordinary black-handled yellow-strawed broom made right here in our belovéd homestate, and she turns her mouth down further and her eyes dance as she says, "Goin to do some sweepin?" and you say yes, wondering why she finds that so god-damned funny, and she looks at the broom again and can barely contain herself and that's when you realize that men in this county don't sweep, or more accurately, they don't sweep with *this* kind of broom; you should have gotten a push-broom, a janitor's broom; but instead, by mistake, you're buying a woman's broom, and you might as well be buying a tube of lipstick or a box of tampons. She takes your money and hands you your change and turns away with her face scrunched up and says "Enjoy your sweepin," and you can't do a thing but say that you will.

DON'T TAKE YOUR hat off inside, even if you're inside a church. Leave it on.

WHEN IT IS 97 degrees and 80% humidity with a heat index of 101 at 5:00 P.M., and you have spent all day digging post holes for 4x4 pressure-treated posts, rough wet wood soaked in arsenic and copper chromate, hallucinogenic fumes of toxicity wafting off them in the staggering heat, and you are choking on concrete dust as you lift and tear and dump the 80-lb bags of Redi-Mix, just add water, and with the side of a hoe you are churning buckets of muddy riverwater into the choking powder until it's a bubbling slurry you can hardly heave and pour toward the posthole, and when you have tried unsuccessfully for the fourth time to lift and set plumb a 12-foot post into the wet concrete, and the two snarky teenagers who will share this house with you are, one, at the beach surfing and two, back in town lying in bed in the air-conditioning watching music videos, then there is nothing you can do except go inside the house you are building for them and stand in the teenagers' rooms, first one and then the other, and spit on their floors.

JEFFERY IS AN idiot, and the reason you know this is because (a), Mr. Hollowell says "I knowed him all my life, and that boy ain't right," and (b), out of nowhere he materializes one afternoon—Jeffery Skittlethorpe, a grownup high school dropout skidding across your muddy yard on a rusted bicycle—to introduce himself and offer his help building the house, and when you ask him how much he would charge he squints at the white noon sky and then stares at his tattered blue bowling shoes and then looks up at you to gauge your expression and then says "Not much" and you ask him "How much" and a little uncertainly he says "How 'bout two dollars an hour?"

INVENT GOOFY NAMES for everything and give them a sardonic twist when saying them aloud. For example, at a used tool shop you find an ancient sledge hammer that some previous owner has painted pink, perhaps to forestall theft (who would want a pink sledge hammer?). Buy this thing and call it "Big Pink" and lisp a bit when asking your wife to hand it to you. You have four other hammers at the building site, so you name each of them: Wafflehead, Steely Dan, Cherry, Little Tap-Tap. In the evocative shadows that dapple the plywood subfloor you artistically arrange these four with Big Pink and a rubber mallet called Condom and take several photos from different angles: your hammer arsenal. In this manner you avoid working on the house.

CALL AN ELECTRICIAN a few months before groundbreaking and ask him to put in a temporary power pole so you can run the necessary tools to cut and drill wood, mix cement and mortar, and maybe play a radio for a bit of diversion. Ask yourself what he really means when he wonders on your answering machine if you're seriously framing the house yourself. Call him back and get his voice mail. Play phone tag for a few weeks. Look in the mirror one morning and say *Fuck it, I'll just build the whole goddamn thing with 14-volt rechargeable hand tools.* When the battery on your circular saw gives out after two hours, reach for your Dad's old snaggle-toothed handsaw and pretend you're Amish.

THE WORD HOUSE comes from the Old English *hus*, derived from the Indo-European *(s)keus*, a word which means "to cover or conceal from the sky." The word *board* is related to the Old French *bord*, the side of a ship, and derives ultimately from the Indo-European *bher*, meaning "to cut." The word *window* is a compound from the Old Norse *vindruga*, *vindr*, wind, and *auga*, an eye: *window*, literally an eye for the wind. Now close the dictionary and go buy some nails.

GO INTO BELDON'S Welding and Hardware, stroll the rows of farm implements, tractor hitches and feed bags and irrigation system replacement valves, dusty iron and steel and aluminum things you cannot discern the purpose of; say "hey" to your Secret Girlfriend behind the counter, feel stupid when she doesn't reply, doesn't nod, just waits, gazing with her brown impassive eyes; tell her that for the lally columns holding up the second story of the house you're building you need two 6x6 quarter-inch steel plates cut and sized and drilled out just so and does she think somebody there can do that for you, and she says with her down-turned mouth "Well, *yeah,* this *is* a *weld*ing shop, you know," and you stand there and think, *It is? I thought it was an idiot shop,* but you don't say it, and all the men sitting around the drink cooler eating their Nabs and swigging Co-Colas look down at the tiled floor grinning and won't meet your eyes because they're idiots, all those idiots sitting around a idiot shop.

FOR SOME REASON all your life you have loved it when instead of "an idiot," people say "*a* idiot," as in "I don't know what got into that boy; I reckon he's just a idiot." So when 85-year-old arthritic Mr. Hollowell from next door climbs out of his gleaming black-and-turquoise Dodge Dakota and hobbles over to the property line and shouts to you the same exact sentence he shouts every single day, *You're comin along real good now, ain'tcha?*, you nod and smile and wave and say to yourself that he may be a idiot. "That man useta be mean as a snake," Jeffery told you once, "but ever since he lost his health he's been right nice to me."

A FOUR-FOOT blacksnake lives under your lumber pile; you saw him one day when lifting the last sheet of plywood. Leave him alone.

YOU SEE A black house in a magazine and read an interview with the owner; he says his neighbors hate his house and he doesn't care. Stop framing your house—tell yourself the roof can wait and you're sick of pounding nails and need a break—and paint your exterior walls black. Sing "I see a red door and I want it painted black" over and over again while slapping your brush against the cedar siding. Think *The neighbors will hate this,* and laugh. Think of names for your house: The Black Box, The Death Star.

THERE IS NO plot to the house, no sequence of causally related events. There is no order, no logical development. It yields no secrets to deconstruction. If there ever was a meaning to it, you can no longer express it. You build. All you are doing is creating an object distinct from the objects around it.

LAYING BRICK IS a stressful occupation, so for comic relief the local brickmasons take to driving by for a look at your concrete block foundation.

YOU GO INTO Beldon's hoping to impress your Secret Girlfriend by asking for a carbide tooth blade for a reciprocating saw, and they tell you she isn't working there anymore, that she "had to" elope over the weekend, that her daddy is fit to be tied 'cause he's way too young to be a grandpa and he's swearing on a stack of Bibles to shoot his new son-in-law on sight, and that the reciprocating saw blades are over there, by the C-clamps. You get rung up and bagged by Miss Myrtle, a palsied old woman who smells like cats. You spend the afternoon hacking out window holes with your new saw—ragged ugly slots in the plywood sheathing, empty eye sockets for a bitter wind.

ONE DROWSY DAY sweet with the scent of swamp magnolias in bloom, your wife and her kids surprise you by toting a picnic out to the house site, where with cries of delight they admire all you've done and ask how long it will be before they can move in, a question you cannot bear to answer honestly. Your wife sets down her wicker basket, lets down her lovely hair, spreads a yellow blanket on the riverbank, and feeds you hummus, olives, tomatoes and bread; the kids get boloney sandwiches and cheese doodles. You eat fresh strawberries for desert and toss the tops in the river and watch black and green turtles float up and nudge them with their snouts as sunset paints your black house orange and pink.

ONE DAY YOU count the months backwards and realize you have been working on the house for almost two years. A little later it strikes you that you have been thinking about the house, imagining it, trying to will it into existence, for the past decade. Then you remember that as a child, you would put yourself to sleep each night designing a house in your head: a big house with lots of secret spaces, trick doors and hidden alcoves, walk-in fireplaces and spiral stairs. You find that you can't remember a time when you *weren't* building a house, and then, with despair, you realize too that you will always be building a house, you will never finish the house, that the house is your life: never quite what you wanted, always a work in progress, a collaboration at times but for the most part solo. One nail, one board, one window, one door at a time.

Luke Whisnant is the author of *Watching TV with the Red Chinese*, a novel, and *Street*, a chapbook of poems. His work has appeared in *Esquire, Arts & Letters, American Short Fiction*, and others, and has been anthologized in *This Is Where We Live: Short Stories by 25 Contemporary North Carolina Writers*, and *Racing Home: New Stories by Award-Winning North Carolina Writers*. Three of his pieces have been reprinted in *New Stories from the South: The Year's Best*. He teaches creative writing and literature at East Carolina University, in Greenville, NC.

www.ingramcontent.com/pod-product-compliance
Lightning Source LLC
Chambersburg PA
CBHW030525260626
47157CB00005B/1887